Diary of a Throwaway Kid

First Edition
Printed in United States of America

ISBN: 979-8-9942044-0-5

For information, permissions requests, or inquiries, contact:
Shannon Tessari

Book design: Stewart A. Williams
Publisher: Shannon Tessari

*This book is dedicated to the nurses and children
of 3K and Zone D – your strength, courage,
and resilience inspired every page.*

No one really sees us. No one listens to us. In many ways, we are invisible, just kind of fade into the background. There are almost a half million of us in the United States. Almost a half million, five hundred thousand. Can you wrap your head around that number? Our numbers are about the same as the population of Raleigh, North Carolina. That's the capital of the state where I was born and have lived my whole life. Who are we, you ask? We are ~~foster~~ throwaway kids.

August 28

For the last two weeks I have been a guest at the pediatric in-patient psychiatric unit of the local hospital. I was discharged last night back to my group home. One of the conditions of my discharge was to start therapy, like immediately. So, I started seeing a new therapist today. Two weeks ago I got into a fight with two of the girls in my group home and got sent to the hospital - and then got thrown into the psych unit. Today I'm lying on a couch in yet another new therapist's office. I'm not crazy, just angry. Like, all the time. You would be too if you had to live my life. I should probably explain.

My name is Pink-Envy Serenity Rogers. I'm pretty sure that Pink-Envy is the name of a perfume that someone famous once wore. My name is just one of the many joys I have endured after being born to a meth addict. I guess it could be worse, she could have named me Chlamydia - I mean, I've heard it's been done. Pink-Envy, ha! My name, at least the hyphenated first name sounds like the stage name for someone who dances around a pole - I'm not that coordinated. I very rarely ever feel serene, so I don't use Serenity. I go by Storm, not super common and it kind of describes the way I always feel - like there's a storm raging inside me. Have you ever stood outside right before a violent thunderstorm? You know how the air feels charged with electricity? The dark clouds build then crash together. Ice crystals and other particles in the clouds collide causing electrical charges. When the charge is too much for the clouds to handle, there is a discharge of lightning. The heat from the lightning expands the air around it creating the shockwave that we mere mortals hear as thunder. That is how I feel on the inside most of the time.

As soon as I turn eighteen, I am changing my name legally. I am fourteen years old now, but was never expected to live through the first day of my life. I was a preemie, born at twenty-nine weeks. I'm not sure if my mom even knew she was pregnant. I weighed less than two pounds and was also addicted to meth. I spent much of the first year of my life in the NICU (Neonatal Intensive Care Unit).

This latest therapist, Jane, is yet another therapist in a long line. I have to admit though, she is a little different than the others. I think she actually listens and pays attention when I talk. I also don't get a judgy vibe from her. Anyway, she asked me to keep a journal. She wants me to write my feelings. She said I could "process" what was happening in my head a little better if I took the time to write my feelings out instead of acting on them. I guess it's supposed to help by having me pour out my emotions onto the page instead of pummeling people's faces. Whatever! I'm not a writer, but I'm willing to try anything she suggests as long as it keeps me out of the hospital or juvie.

August 29

Jane asked me to talk to her about what sent me to the hospital. You know, it's funny. The day that I got sent to the hospital about fifteen different people asked me to tell them what brought me to the hospital. Being a natural smartass, my first response was, "the police." Apparently that was not the answer they were looking for. The ER doc who came in to talk to me was a tad bit dramatic. Don't get me wrong, for an old guy, he was pretty hot, but good grief! He gave me the whole, "We can't help you if you won't talk to us" bit. I'm pretty sure he was having a sense of humor failure. I'm guessing that's not something that can be treated in the emergency department. When he left my room, he threw his hands up in the air and said, "I don't understand these kids today. Somebody try to make her talk."

I could see him leaning up against the desks in the nurses' station. He even at one point had this whole "Woe is me" thing going on with his fingers massaging his temples. I saw a wedding ring on his hand. I sure hope he doesn't have kids! If he ever has girls, he might as well check himself into a psych unit throughout their teenage years. Otherwise, he will never survive!

When he walked out, the woman I think is the head nurse was making fun of him. She actually did a really good impersonation. I mean, the back of her hand to her forehead leaning against the station. I heard her say, "The only other thing he needed to do was faint because of the vapors! He really is a bit of a diva."

I have talked about what I had to agree to so the hospital would discharge me and the group home would take me back, but I haven't explained what happened, this time, to send me to the hospital. I was having a bad day. That's always what starts it. When I am having a bad day, I need time alone. I always put myself in a time out because I know I have a temper and I lash out. So, the day I was sent to the hospital I really wanted to be left alone, but two of the other girls, Female and Fantasia started picking on me about my name. Really? Female (pronounced fa-ma-lay)? Her mom was too stupid to realize that was the sex of the baby, not its name?

The story Female tells is that her mom saw her in the nursery, saw the nametag on the bassinet that read "Female Martin" and thought the nurses named the baby for her. Don't even get me started on Fantasia, or as I call her, Fangtasia because of her messed up teeth. She has two front teeth that look like they could have been stolen from Bugs Bunny. Her bottom teeth are so crowded together they look as though they grew in sideways.

Some of them look really sharp, like fangs. Her mouth looks like a rabbit and angler fish mated. It is really scary!

Anyway, so they started teasing me about my name, "Ooh, Pink-Envy, wit a name like at, you should be clappin' cheeks out there on the corner."

I told Fangtasia she was just jealous because with her mouth, no guy would ever want to get close to her - I mean like ever. She'd be a pecker wrecker for sure! She came at me with her claws. But I fight dirty. I'm small so I was able to get around her, jump on her back and start choking her out while I yanked out her extensions. Female stood there screaming. Fangtasia finally slammed me back into the wall. I hit my head and let go. By the time the staff got to us, they were both crying and carrying on.

The group home staff called for the police and an ambulance and said that I had to go. They saw some scratches on my arms, caused by Fangtasia, and said it was a suicide attempt. If they had actually looked harder, they could have seen that they were scratches! I mean, yeah, I am bleeding on the inside of my right wrist, but it's from where Fangtasia put her nails through my skin when she was trying to get away from me.

None of the adults would listen to anything I had to say. They also told the police that I was the primary attacker, and the other girls were simply defending themselves. Of course, none of the staff were anywhere close enough to see or hear what happened, but I have a reputation as a troublemaker, and it was two against one. There was no way my side of the story was going to be heard.

I was pretty sure when they hauled me away that I would never be allowed to come back to this group home. Not that it would have broken my heart. The staff all seem to hate me, and I don't get along with any of the kids, but as long as I continue to see Jane, I am allowed to stay. Yay, me!

August 30

Jane has a suggested list of writing prompts I could use. Or I could just write. Today, I just want to write. I play a game when I go into new situations like new group homes, foster homes, or the hospital. I act like I'm really tough and not afraid of anything. If I don't show any fear, no one will come after me. I pretty much liked all the nurses this time around. They were pretty nice. I was scared a lot, so one of the nurses brought me coloring pages and crayons.

I don't understand why I am brought to the psych unit when I act out. I mean, I know that I have all these different alphabet soup diagnoses after my name (ODD, oppositional defiant disorder, RAD, reactive attachment disorder, and possibly ADHD, attention deficit hyperactivity disorder), but none of them have been cured by the medication I take. I'm pretty sure the "mood disorder" diagnoses I've been stuck with are just code for, "She's an asshole." All of my experiences, though, have led me to believe that the hospital doesn't have a cure for the common asshole. I have been on a wide variety of medications, most of them don't do anything other than make me feel really sluggish. Sometimes I feel like there's way too much medicine and I just want to be a normal kid.

I bet there are kids out there who have never taken Ritalin, Adderall, or Vyvanse. Those are just a few of the meds I've been on. Anyway, the psych unit always scares me. I have been told that if it bothers me so much, then maybe I should just stop acting out.

"Use your coping skills," they say.

"What are those?" I ask.

The psych unit has these sitters. I don't think they're called babysitters, but it's basically the same thing. Anyway, the sitters are these people who sit in your doorway and watch you. That's it. That's their whole job, just watching. They watch me sleep, they watch me eat, they even watch when I go to the bathroom. I'm not suicidal so I don't get it. It's really embarrassing. I guess it could be worse. In one of the units that I was on, one of the girls was a huge suicide risk. I mean, they wouldn't even let her have a plastic straw because there was one time where she had one and turned it into a weapon. She found a way to slit her wrist with it.

She ended up having to have surgery to repair what she had done. When she came back to our unit, the rule was zero privacy for her. She couldn't even take a shower without a sitter being in the bathroom to observe her! At least I can take a shower without someone watching.

My most recent visit, right after Female, Fangtasia, and I had our meeting of the minds, I walked by a room where a woman's body was jerking all over the place and she was yelling at the nurses. It scared me because it reminded me of one of my only memories of my mother. She had overdosed on meth and was jerking all over just like this woman was. Mama died when I was four. She had just turned twenty.

I found a picture of Mama at my grandma's house. It was hidden in the back of a book in the room that had once been Mama's. I stole the picture and hid it with my things. I still had it hidden when I was taken away from Grandma. Mama was beautiful before meth. I saw a movie once called "The Help." There was an actress in there that none of the other ladies liked. I thought she was beautiful. The actress's name was Jessica Chastain. Mama looked a lot like her before the meth. By the time she died, she looked like one of those creatures stumbling around in "The Walking Dead."

—

The night I fought with Female and Fangtasia when EMS and the police brought into the emergency department, the unit I was placed in was shaped like an "L" and the first room I was in was on the backside of the nurses' station where the nurse aides worked. After the doctor left, one of the nurse aides told me I was going to have to strip out of my clothes and put on their scrubs. I wasn't wearing any jewelry, so that wasn't a problem. Even though I had been through this a bunch of times, I still hated that they had to watch me change. The worst part of it is when they ask you to pull down your underwear, squat and cough. I understand why they have to do it, but damn!

After I changed they swabbed my nose - they said they tested everyone for COVID as a precaution, just in case there was a possibility that the patient would be admitted. Heaven forbid they admit a sick person into the hospital! Then they drew blood. By this point I really wasn't listening. They had asked me way too many questions and I felt violated. I was waiting for the body cavity search.

The first night I was there I was in a room that looked out at the nurses' station. My room was also right next to the meth head. She kept shouting out words and sounds that made no sense. There was so much noise in the unit, it was overwhelming. There was a man in another room who kept yelling "Everything!" at the top of his lungs.

Then the woman across the hall from me started to have a meltdown. My guess is that the noise got to be a little too much for her, too. A nurse went in to give her some medication. I think it was meant to help her calm down. She smacked the nurse's hand, and the pills went flying everywhere.

Before I could blink there were security guards everywhere. There was an overhead page announcing a security alert. There was so much noise, I could almost feel the vibrations of the sound waves pulsing in the air. The head nurse charged down the hall with two shots in her hands. I could hear her over the rest of the commotion.

She yelled, "Becky, I don't have the time or the patience for this tonight."

I could see six guards in the room. Each of the guards looked as though they could have been Dwayne Johnson's body doubles. There was at least one guard on each of Becky's limbs, one of them was holding her head to keep her from biting. Meanwhile there were three nurses attaching restraint straps to the frame of the bed. After the straps were secured to the bed, each of Becky's four limbs were wrestled into a strap.

The woman on the bed started screaming even louder, "You fucking bitch. I didn't want those shots. I told you I didn't want any medicine!" Then she started crying. Her screams got louder as the men started forcing her wrists and feet into restraints. She kept screaming, "You're hurting me, please stop hurting me. Why are you doing this to me? Get the fuck off of me! I am going to sue every last one of you!" After she was restrained, she kept screaming and pulling at the restraints.

The blonde nurse said, "Becky, stop fighting us! You're getting the medicine you need to help you calm down. This will help you!"

The lady in the bed was screaming louder and louder. It sounded like she was being attacked.

She shouted, "What the fuck are you giving me?"

The nurse said, "You are getting fifty milligrams of Benadryl, five milligrams of haloperidol, and two milligrams of lorazepam."

"No!! No, no, no! I do not want a B-fifty-two!"

The screaming grew louder then stopped suddenly. After the screaming stopped, I heard the woman sobbing.

I curled into as small a ball as I could in the bed. I didn't cover my head, because I knew that wasn't allowed, but I didn't want anyone to see me – I was really scared and I had started crying. The sitter called one of the nurses over and whispered something to her. The next thing I know, I'm moving to a new room at the end of the hall. The head nurse, who comes across as really tough and inflexible, I think secretly, really cares. I think she puts off that hard shell to protect herself from caring too much.

She told me, "I'm going to move you to this end of the hallway for now to keep you further away from some of the noise. It can get very loud in here at times."

It was quieter at the end of the hallway. Much quieter! I was able to curl up and go to sleep.

August 31

Writing prompt: *If you could change one thing about yourself what would it be?*

That's an easy one. I would change the family I was born into. My mom is dead. She overdosed on meth and fentanyl when I was four. Adding insult to injury, while she was smoking her fentanyl-laced meth, her boyfriend gave me acid. I was four, and he had me dropping acid! To be fair, I'm not sure that he truly meant to give me drugs. He had been smoking with Mama and was pretty high, too. Meth and fentanyl were their drugs of choice, but every so often, they liked to expand their horizons and drop acid.

I discovered long after their drugs days that there are many different ways that people get high on acid. One of the most common is putting several drops on sugar cubes. Once it's swallowed, the drug gets released into the body, and you get your high. Mama and her boyfriend had been putting their drops of acid on sweet tarts and taking it that way. When I went to her boyfriend and begged him for some candy, he handed me a sweet tart. Maybe without realizing it, he had just allowed a four-year-old to drop acid. Brilliant guy. I was probably having the Dumbo pink elephants on parade experience when he realized there was something wrong with my mom.

I don't remember much about that day. I have weird memories with lots of colors and weird shapes. I know that we were both taken to the hospital. My mom died that day. I was really too young to remember much about her and the memories that I have are fuzzy. Anyway, she died and no one was ever really sure who my father was. That's when I went to live with my hyper-religious grandmother.

That was a real treat. I'm pretty sure her favorite Bible verse was "Spare the rod and spoil the child." The rod was almost never spared in her home.

Before Mama died, she, her boyfriend and I had lived in a dirty, run down single wide trailer in a place called Shoofly. Shoofly is a small town that isn't really a town outside of a really small town called Stem in North Carolina. My grandmother lived in Stem, not too far from where the trailer was. I mean, I'm pretty sure we were less than a five-minute drive from the trailer to Grandma's house. When Mama ran away pregnant at sixteen, Grandma told her not to come back. What I remember being told was that Grandma told her she was trash and should go live in the heap with the rest of the losers.

I remember thinking how old my grandmother was. In reality, she wasn't yet forty and could have easily passed me off as her own daughter, but Granville County was a small place and everyone who knew her, also knew my mama. Grandma had gotten married at eighteen and immediately got pregnant – or so she says. Plenty of people think that Grandma had to get married because she was pregnant.

I was discharged from the hospital to a sheriff's deputy who drove me to my grandmother's house. To this day I don't know why she couldn't be bothered to come to the hospital to get me herself. Shortly after the deputy dropped me off at Grandma's, she took me by the hand and walked me outside. We went to this huge weeping willow that was in the center of her backyard. She told me to pick my switch. I didn't know what that meant. We picked it out together. Our first bonding moment together and we were in the backyard cutting the switch that would later be used on my bottom at any perceived wrong. This way, she could be sure that I would never become spoiled. Grandma had a hall tree with a bench in the entryway of her house. She placed my switch on the top and told me that from now on, this was going to be called the whipping post.

We went to church every Sunday. All of Grandma's friends gathered around her telling her what a saint she was for taking me in. Grandma got me set up in the Jesus Loves Me little ones Bible study. It was more like daycare during the service where the little ones got to color Biblically themed coloring pages. One Sunday after I had been living with Grandma for about a month, I had an accident. The teacher for the four-year-old classroom took me to the bathroom to clean me up. While she was cleaning me, she saw my bottom and part of my lower back. She kept asking me, "Is someone hurting you?"

I answered, "If you spare the rod, you spoil the child."

About a week later, a social worker showed up at the house. My few belongings were quickly gathered, placed in a garbage bag and I left with the social worker. I haven't seen Grandma since.

I look at some of the other kids I go to school with, the ones who still live with their real parents and I wonder. I have to have done something bad in a past life or something to have ended up the way I have. Maybe I was a really bad baby, and this is God's way of punishing me. I read somewhere that the Buddha taught that desire is the source of all suffering. My guess is that it's true because I desire a real, loving family. I don't remember the last time I didn't feel like I was suffering.

september 1

I had another session with Jane today. I really like her. We talked about the safety plan that I wrote up with the nurse before I was discharged from the hospital. Jane wanted to work through each point of the behavior plan to make sure I really understood what they were looking for. I was really pissy at first. I told her, "I'm not an idiot." I could feel my temper starting to flare.

She told me she knew that I wasn't an idiot. Then she told me to notice my feelings. She said she could tell that I was getting angry because my face had gotten red and I was clenching my fists. She calmly asked me if I knew how I felt right before a crisis. Could I tell what was happening with my body right before I totally lost it? I must have had a look of confusion on my face because she said, "When you went to the hospital the last time, why did they send you?"

I told her, "Because I got into a fight with Female and Fangtasia."

She unsuccessfully tried to stifle a giggle. "Storm, her name is Fantasia. You were mad because she was making fun of your name, yet here you continue to poke fun at hers."

"To be fair, I'm making fun of her teeth, not her name."

Jane pursed her lips, looked at me very pointedly and raised her eyebrows. "Not funny, Storm. I really want to get through this plan with you today."

"Okay," I said. "I'm sorry. They just bug me. What do you want me to do?"

Jane said, "Think back to the moments right before the fight. How were you feeling – think beyond just angry. Can you remember how your body felt? If you need to close your eyes to put yourself back there, you can. Sometimes, I have to do that, too."

"You're in therapy?" I asked, astonished.

"Not about me, but yes, I see a therapist. Sometimes I need help sorting out my feelings, too. Now, let's get back to you."

I closed my eyes and put myself back in the common room on the afternoon that I fought with Female and Fang, sorry Fantasia. I could feel my heart rate starting to pick up. I also felt my face suddenly flush with heat. I started to feel my muscles contracting so that I could jump into action. I felt the swarm of butterflies in my stomach as my adrenaline kicked in. The last sensation I felt was a cold prickling sensation across my scalp and down the back of my neck. For me, that sensation always comes when I know I'm about to do something really stupid, and I'll probably get caught, and get into really big trouble. In my head I played out the entire scene with Female and Fantasia.

It went a lot slower than it had when it was really happening.

I was relaying all of this to Jane as I was going through it. When I opened my eyes and looked at her, she had a big smile on her face.

"You did it!" Jane was so excited. "So, you remember the adrenaline rush you felt right before you jumped on Fantasia's back?"

"Is that what that was?"

"Yes, your fight or flight instincts kicked in. I want to work on coping skills – things you can do to help curb that feeling so you don't go into attack mode."

"I don't know any coping skills." I was ashamed to say it, but it was true. I had no idea how to calm myself down when I got mad. I was one of those babies who couldn't self-soothe. I chalk it up to my prenatal meth use.

Jane said to me, "Most kids don't know coping skills. To be fair, there are a lot of adults walking around who have never developed coping skills. It's not something you are instinctively born with. Part of the parenting job is to teach these skills. It's also something that can be learned in therapy. It's never too late to learn."

"Okay," I said. "So, teach me."

Jane spent the rest of our time together working with me on coping skills. The breathing techniques didn't seem to be all that useful. I thought something like running or swimming was going to be better for me, but I really didn't think the group home was going to allow me to go for a run when I was mad.

What Jane and I landed on was yoga. I discovered that some of the poses could be really challenging. That created a physical outlet, and also forced me to use some of the breathing that she had tried to teach me. At the end of our session when the group home supervisor came to pick me up, Jane talked her about how important it was to allow me to put myself into a time-out when I started to feel angry.

I really want this to work. I don't like living in the group home, but I've already been bounced around a bunch this year. I'd like not to have to move again. If I do have to move, it would be nice to be moved to a foster family where I have a chance for adoption. That is my dream. It probably isn't realistic, but I would love to have a real family, maybe a brother and sister, or a brother or sister. Nice parents. And a dog. They have to have a dog. I don't think that's too much to ask.

september 2

My prompt for today was, *what am I afraid of and how is it limiting me?*

What I'm afraid of is that I will continue to bounce from home to home and never actually belong anywhere. At the ripe old age of fourteen, I have already been in nine foster homes, and three group homes. I have been in these places called PRTFs. That stands for Psychiatric Residential Treatment Facility. I got sent to one of those because the foster parents I lived with when I was twelve convinced a psychiatrist that I was bipolar.

I will admit that I was kind of all over the place and moody when I was twelve. That was when my period started. Of course I was moody! It probably didn't help that I didn't like the family I was living with at the time. The parents were okay, but they had two bio kids who were total brats! Absolutely the worst! Their girls were fourteen and sixteen and I think they were a little pissed that their parents decided to foster another girl.

They might have been okay with a boy – they probably wouldn't have messed with him the way they did with me.

It started off small. They would tease me, or pick on me, but they would always make sure their parents weren't in the room and couldn't hear what was happening. They would push and push and push until I would explode and start yelling. Of course, that would happen when their parents were close by and could see and hear everything.

Then they started hiding my things. Foster kids don't have much, especially those of us who go from home to home. What we do have is typically sent from one place to the next in a trash bag, so it has to be light enough for us to carry on our own. The things that we do keep with us may not have much value to anyone but us, but to us, it's treasure. My greatest treasure was a photo album that had pictures of me and my mom. It's all I had left of her.

I had a few stuffed animals that I had carried with me. One had been with me since I was two or three. It's an old Winnie the Pooh bear. Anyway, after I freaked out on them one afternoon for teasing me, I started to notice things were either moved or missing from my room. One time it was a hairbrush, another time I couldn't find my socks. Then they started messing around with my stuffed animals.

We were required to make our beds every morning before we left for school. When I make my bed, I always put Pooh bear in the middle. I also have a stuffed elephant and a stuffed wolf. The elephant goes to his right and the wolf goes to his left. I don't know why, it's just the way I've always done it. One day, I came home after school and found the stuffed animals in the wrong spots. I know that sounds like a silly thing to get upset about, but these were the only things that were truly mine – and these girls who had everything were coming into my space and touching my things.

When Pooh bear went missing, I had a meltdown. I searched everywhere in my room. When I still couldn't find him, I started searching through the fourteen-year-old's room. Their parents caught me after I had searched under the bed and was starting to throw things out of the hope chest at the end of her bed. They punished me by taking the remaining stuffed animals away from me for the rest of the week. When the week ended, miraculously, all three of my stuffed animals were waiting for me on my bed when I got home from school.

The final straw for me was when my photo album went missing. I always kept the album in the drawer of my nightstand. One of my nighttime rituals was taking out the album and looking through it right before bed. I don't have a lot of memories of my mom, so sometimes I made up stories to go with the pictures. Grandma was never able to tell me what had been going on in the pictures because she wasn't there for any of it, so I created my own memories.

My last night in their home, I opened my nightstand and the album was gone. I looked around the nightstand, then got out of bed and searched on the floor, and under the bed. I went through every drawer in the dresser, then went into my closet.

When I couldn't find it, I went to the fourteen-year-old's room. I didn't bother knocking on her door, I just went in.

"Where is it?" I demanded.

She smiled sweetly at me and said, "Where is what?"

"My photo album. Where is it?"

She said, "I have no idea what you are talking about."

She was sitting in her bed and showed no intention of getting up, so I went to her dresser and started to dump the contents of each of her drawers onto the floor.

She screamed and launched herself at me from the bed. "Get out of my room!" She flew at me with both hands looking like talons, like she was going to try to either rip out my hair or claw my eyes.

I punched her hard in the stomach and knocked the wind out of her. When her older sister came flying into the room, I turned on her and screamed. "Where is it?"

"You hit her!"

By this point, my rage had reached a critical level. I couldn't think anymore, the storm inside me was so violent I felt wild and out of control. I wasn't even looking for the photo album anymore. I was just tearing up the room. I was the storm. I had ripped posters off the wall and swiped everything that had been on the dresser onto the floor. The older sister came up behind me and grabbed me to try and get me under control. That was a mistake. I slammed my head back into her face and broke her nose.

The parents came into the room and saw the destruction

that I had done, found their youngest curled on the floor with her arms wrapped around her stomach, crying. Their oldest daughter was also crying. She had grabbed a T-shirt and was trying to stop the blood that was gushing from her shattered nose.

Not even an hour later, I was sitting on the front porch with all of my belongings in a trash bag waiting for someone from DSS to come pick me up. The family let me know that in no uncertain terms was I *ever* allowed to come back into their house. They left me out on the porch unsupervised. I don't know that they would have cared if I had run away before the social worker got there to collect me. They were done with me, and I'm sure any future plans for fostering.

And biggest surprise of all, my stuffed animals and photo album didn't make it into the garbage bag.

—

I had to go back and reread the prompt because I kind of got lost in that memory. What I am most afraid of is that I will never find a family that will want me forever. I think all foster kids dream at some point about their forever family. How is it limiting me? I don't really think my fear is limiting me. I think what's limiting me is me.

september 3

I'm back in the hospital. I tried so hard to use my coping skills. I really did. I tried the meditation thing, I tried to distance myself. I even put myself in time out when I started getting mad. Yesterday I was doing a yoga video from YouTube. The thing about it is that I was in MY room! I wasn't hurting anyone. I wasn't even in anyone's way. My roommate, Luna, was in the common room watching TV. One of the videos I'd seen earlier had talked about connecting the breath with the movement. I thought that since I was calm and in a good mood I would go ahead and practice – that way it would be easier to use the breathing exercises when I started getting mad.

I was warming up with sun salutations and felt something hit me hard on the back of the head. I turned around and there they were: Female and Fangtasia.

Fangtasia looked really pissed, "Bitch, you pulled out my hair. You gonna die!"

Female just stood there smiling like she was enjoying the

scene. Fangtasia pulled a knife on me, "Grab her!" The two of them rushed me. I wasn't fast enough this time to get into a good position to fight. I was able to knock the knife out of her hand before she swung it at my face. I still caught her fist under my chin. The blow was hard enough to make my jaw snap shut. It felt like my teeth should have shattered. I'm just glad my tongue wasn't in the way – I'm pretty sure I would have lost it. Female had run around to the other side of the bed and was grabbing at my wrists. Fangtasia got up off me and hesitated just a second too long. I pulled my knees into my chest and then kicked out as hard as I could, catching her in the center of her chest. She went flying backward over Luna's bed.

Female let go of my wrists and ran to check on Fantasia, who had hit her head on the doorframe during her flight.

That was when Darnella, the group home supervisor, chose to show up. She glared at me while pulling her phone out of her back pocket. "Girl, you done here.

"Darnella, I didn't do anything but defend myself." I screamed in frustration. I really wanted her to listen to me, but she was already talking to a 911 dispatcher saying she needed police and EMS. I didn't care if I got shipped off to another new place, but I really didn't want the new place to have the idea that I was violent before I even got there.

The next thing I knew, the police and EMS were there. I was getting strapped into a gurney and the medic was trying to play Billy Badass.

He got up in my face and asked me, "Are you going to be a

problem for me? If you are, we can go ahead and restrain you right now. Just give me an excuse to give you the juice!"

I glared at him, but said very quietly, "I'm not going to give you any trouble."

As the medics were rolling me out of my room, Darnella was going in with garbage bags to "pack" my things. The last group home I was in, the house supervisor threw all my stuff into a garbage bag and left it on the front porch for DSS to come get it. By the time they got there, half of my stuff was gone because the other girls in the house had gone through it and taken whatever they wanted. I'm pretty sure that's what's going to happen this time, too.

They loaded me onto the ambulance and slammed the doors shut. I did my best to curl myself into a ball and sleep. I hoped no one noticed that I was crying.

———

The hospital staff put me in the same room I was in last time. We went through the same drill. They took blood from me, did a covid swab, and made me pee in a cup, and made me change into their prison garb. I know it's really just scrubs, but I swear if I had broken the law and was being sent to jail, I'm pretty sure I'd have more rights. I can't even wear my bra. It is so embarrassing to have to walk around with everything hanging out. Like usual, all of my stuff was taken, but they did let me keep my journal.

It is so cold in this room! I can only have one blanket and

there is no way to adjust the air conditioner. I realize it's almost a hundred degrees outside, but it feels like the inside of a fridge in here. I feel like there are icicles forming on my nose. The blanket feels gross. It's this thick, weird material that is not cozy AT ALL! I think it's one of those psych safe blankets that can't rip so the rest of the inmates here can't kill themselves. I don't really care, I just wish I could warm up.

september 4

I waited for hours for the psychiatrist to come talk to me last night. Apparently, there was no one available in person, so I got to talk to a doc in a box. One of the nurse aides brought this huge television screen on wheels into my room. That was how I was evaluated. The psychiatrist talked to me from a television screen. He told me he thinks I might have some trouble with impulse control and anger management. This isn't exactly news to me. I've been hearing about this my whole life. Lack of impulse control and poor frustration management is just another gift that keep on giving. Thank you, Mama for getting me addicted to meth in the womb.

I asked this morning if I could call Jane. I thought it might help me to talk to someone who I think really cares about me. The nurse told me that the only person I'm allowed to call, or receive calls from, is my legal guardian. I wish they understood that my legal guardian is some woman in Granville County that I met a couple of times ten years ago. That woman doesn't know me. I am just a case file number to her.

Today there are several other kids here as patients. They were trying to make room for more in the main psych area, so they moved six of us to this even more depressing area of the emergency room.. The way this area is set up, there are two rooms with three of us to a room. We each have a recliner and there is a bathroom. The nurse sits in a locked office area.

There are two other girls sitting over here with me and three boys in the other room. I think we all probably qualify as throwaway kids. I don't think any of them actually live with their parents anymore. The girls in the room with me have been living in the same group home together for a while. They seem to know each other really well. The one girl's name is Izzy, the other is Rumor. When I asked about her name, she told me her mom is a really huge Bruce Willis fan and she and her sisters are named after his daughters.

Everyone here has a story. Izzy and Rumor were sent here because they walked away from their group home to go meet some random boy. Izzy had found a way to bypass the internet restrictions her group home had set up and was talking to a bunch of different people online. She had set up a meeting with this one guy she thought was really cute and begged Rumor to go with her. They must have walked around for hours. They went to this park where he was supposed to meet her but he never showed up. When it started getting dark, they knocked on doors. There was one house where when they knocked, a woman answered the door and brought them in. She called the police then sat them down to try to explain to them how dangerous it was to do what they were doing. Long story short, their behavior was considered to be unacceptable, so they were brought to the hospital.

september 5

I spend most of my time in here sleeping. It's so depressing. The only thing there is to do is watch movies or sleep. I don't really have much interest in the movies they want to watch. Every so often Izzy and Rumor tried to talk to me. They seem really nice, but I don't want to make friends here. I just want to find out where I'm going next and find a way to survive until I turn eighteen and can get out of this system. Maybe when I am discharged, I can look up how to become an emancipated minor.

september 6

The most exciting thing that happened today was two of the boys in the other section of this dungeon started getting loud like they were about to fight. Security was called and they were moved. I asked the nurse if I could have something to help me with anxiety. She gave me some Ativan so I'm going to sleep now. I really hate this recliner.

september 11

I can't remember what the nurse told me she gave me, but it made me sleep for the better part of two days. After that, I just didn't feel like writing. Izzy and Rumor have gone back to their group home. They were welcomed back. I am still waiting for placement. It sucks being the kid no one wants. I think most of the boys have gone somewhere else, too.

The nurse today is really nice. She told me they are trying to get me into a bed in the pediatric inpatient unit. You know, I don't want to die, but sometimes I wish I could go to sleep, not wake up and simply live in my dreams. The good dreams. It would be nice to fall asleep and fall into a dream where this life that I've been living is not the real one. In my dream, my real life would be amazing! I would have a mom who loves to cook and bake and spend time with me. I would have a dad for real. Maybe he would be the kind of dad who would have taken me to a daddy daughter dance when I was little. Even though I'm fourteen, he would be the kind of daddy who would still call me princess. And I wouldn't have such a lame name.

I asked the nurse if there were any books that I could read. If I can't lose myself in a dreamworld I would kill to lose myself in something other than the reality TV crap that has been on endlessly! I even switched the TV to MTV, but the only thing playing there was *Ridiculousness*. To me, that whole show is ridiculous and a waste of good air time. I heard one of the nurses say she remembers when MTV, music television, actually used to have music videos. Huh, imagine that!

Oh my gosh! The nurse found a book for me! *The Secret Garden*! I have always loved that book.

september 12

So, I heard from my legal guardian yesterday. Her name is Jasmine Williamson. I am just another "case" for her. I was assigned to her a couple years ago, but I've only met her a few times. She told me I will be moving to a new group home some-time in the next week. I was okay with it until I found out that I'll be moving to a totally different part of the state. This last group home was in Durham. My new group home will be in a town called Sylva in Jackson County. That is way out in the mountains. It's scary to think about moving away from what I have always known, but I guess it won't be too bad. I've always liked being out in nature. Maybe the group home will have a yard with a lot of trees. I could pretend I'm Katniss Everdeen fighting for the survival of District Twelve.

The nurses moved me back to the behavioral health portion of the emergency room where I started. There is a very unpleas-ant girl over here. I kind of wish they would have her go over to the locked area. She walked on to the unit today, trailed by the medics from EMS. She snapped her fingers above her head and announced, "Hey, bitches I'm back!"

I watched the reactions from the nurses as she strutted across the unit. She acted as though she were royalty and was expecting her loyal subjects of the emergency department to shower her with adoration. One of the nurses cringed and shuddered. Another one just shook her head and turned her chair around.

The head nurse just looked at her and yelled, "Tyquanna, what are you doing back here? I thought the last time was going to be the last time."

She replied, "I got into a fight with Tynisha. She was acting like the bitch she is and started trying to tell me what to do. I told her fat, ugly ass to go jump in traffic and kill herself before I killed her. Mama heard us fighting and called the cops."

The head nurse shook her head in disgust. I overheard the other nurses and the aides talking about how they were going to wait until the doctor came to see her before they started her triage process since she was always there. One of them asked, "When is DSS going to do something about this family?"

Well, if my life is any indication of how successful DSS a intervention can be, they will not only continue to deal with these children in their intact family, but they will also deal their children's children.

september 13

For the first time in ten days, I get to wear my own clothing! It seems like such a little thing, but just making that change out of the hospital issued scrubs has made a huge difference in the way I feel. I had all of my things together and was waiting on the social worker to pick me up when I saw the head nurse was working. I have to wonder if she ever goes home, it feels like she is here all day, every day. I wanted to thank her for being so nice to me. She really went out of her way to make sure that I felt cared for and comfortable – all of the nurses did, really.

A Jackson County social worker came to take me to my new group home. She said it would take about four hours to get where we're going so I hoped I got to read and write most of the way. She drove a Subaru Outback and told me that I could recline the backseat a little if I wanted to. I really just wanted to read. That must have been okay with her, because as soon as she got into the car, she shoved some air pods into her ears and didn't speak to me again the entire trip. Is it even legal to drive while listening to air pods or headphones? If it isn't is should be.

I read my book from the time we pulled out of the hospital parking lot until we were just past a town called Statesville. She had taken Interstate forty, which would be the fastest route. After Statesville, there was just too much to see. We crossed over a large river that had several expensive looking boats lazily cruising by. Shortly after crossing over the river, I saw my first glimpse of the North Carolina foothills. The site of those hills in the background was thrilling for me. I felt a longing to explore their beauty that was almost as strong as my desire for a family.

Thirty minutes later I understood why the Western Carolina mountains are called "smoky." The cloud cover was so thick, it felt as though I could reach my hand out the window and pull a piece away like I was pulling on cotton candy. I didn't try it, I thought it might make me look stupid, but I was very tempted. By the time we got to the group home, the sun was starting to set. The low hanging clouds helped to produce an amazingly stunning backdrop for the house. The riot of colors started with a white/yellow center that gradually warmed to the slightest orange. The orange bled its colors a little deeper, turning the sky pink, then almost red. Just over the peaks of the mountains, the fog that clung to the mountains looking like smoke was a violet blue – the same shade of blue seen in the hottest portion of the flame on a Bunsen burner. It was breathtaking! And this was going to be my new home.

Then I noticed the house. It was enormous! The outside looked as though it needed to be power washed and painted, but the house was nicer than anyplace I'd ever lived. It looked like an early 1900s farmhouse with beige siding and a green metal roof. There was a brick walkway that led to a bricked porch. The porch had a wide overhang and six rocking chairs placed so they were in pairs slanted toward each other. The owner had strung decorative lights across the front of the porch. Each light was in the shape of a dragonfly. There were carriage lights on either side of the red front door, which had been left open, inviting me to come in.

I looked at the social worker with a silent request for permission to enter. She grinned and said, "Go ahead. They're waiting for you."

I opened the glass storm door and was drawn farther into the house by the aromas coming from the kitchen. It didn't matter that I had never been here before, I was able to follow my nose. I could hear what sounded like a lot of people all talking and laughing together. Right inside the door was a large staircase. To the right of the staircase was the dining room. There was a table there big enough to fit ten chairs around it! I can't remember a time when I ever ate with a family at a table.

I came around the corner a little more and saw there was a huge fireplace and beyond that there was a huge kitchen with what looked like a very happy family gathered around the counters. I counted one teenaged boy, three teenaged girls and a little boy, probably no more than five. Then I saw the adults, my new foster parents. They all worked together to make dinner. There was a jumble of conversation and joking, then the teenaged boy turned my way and stopped talking mid-sentence. I froze and everyone else went silent.

The social worker, I probably should have paid more attention to her name but, oh well, she came up behind me and said, "Storm, this is Mr. and Mrs. McClelland. Robert, Ann, this is Storm."

Mrs. McClelland came over to me and gave me a warm hug. It really took me by surprise. I am not much of a huggy type of person, but it just felt right. She has long brownish blonde hair that had been pulled back in a ponytail and she looks like an athlete. She smells the way I have always thought moms are supposed to smell – like vanilla and sunshine. I'm not really sure how else to explain it, but it sure is nice!

When she was finished hugging me, she kept her arm around my shoulders and her hand on my arm. "Storm, let me introduce you to the rest of the family. This is Cadence."

Cadence is tall and super skinny. She looks to be about my age. She has beautiful long brown hair that goes all the way down to her waist. She is really pale, too. I wonder if she is sick. She reminds me of a breakable porcelain doll. She's really pretty in a very fragile way.

The next kid was about five. He had pushed his way to the front of the group then stood there staring at me. He had coppery red hair and freckles all over his face. His eyes were bright blue. He was wearing what looked like a shirt full of dirt and food stains and denim shorts. Mrs. McClelland said, "This is Brian. The tall guy over there is Erik, and the girls at the stovetop cooking are Chloe and Zoe."

I was so overwhelmed I had no idea what to say. I could feel my face heating p and turning bright red so I ducked my head, waved, and barely whispered, "Hi."

Mrs. McClelland said, "Brian, why don't you show Storm where the dishes are so she can set herself a place at the table. Storm, here we all eat as a family. I don't know what you're used to, but we want you to feel like you are one of us as long as you are here – which I hope will be permanently."

Little Brian came running over and grabbed my hand. He didn't say anything, just tugged on my arm to follow him. I got the dish and the silverware and we all sat down to eat. I have no idea when the social worker left. There had been such a flurry of activity around my arrival at dinnertime that everything has kind of blurred together. I wish I could have thanked her for bringing me here. Today has been one of the best days of my entire life.

september 14

I was so tired last night I'm pretty sure I was asleep before I got into my bed. This place is awesome! Everyone was very warm and welcoming last night. I found out that all of the kids here are foster kids – like, this is not actually a group home, but a foster home. And all of the kids say that this is a great place to be. The McClellands have been taking in foster kids for years. Erik told me that there are older kids who the McClellands adopted who come back to visit every so often. In fact, the McClellands are going through the process of adopting Erik now. He is really lucky!

He told me that they don't force the adoptions on the kids they foster. They want the kids to want to live with them. He said that he only knows of a couple of kids who turned them down when they offered the adoption route. According to Erik, the kids who didn't want to be adopted, continued to live with them as fosters, but held onto the hope that one day their families would get their shit together and come for them. Even those kids still come to visit. Erik said that one of the magical things about the McClellands is that they don't just boot the kids out the door they day they turn eighteen. They give them the chance to find their way, then help them moved on when they are ready. They sound too good to be true!

Dinner last night was some of the best food I have ever had. Mrs. McClelland was teaching the twins – Chloe and Zoe – how to cook Italian food. She had made this dish she called stuffed shells. I have never had anything like it. I asked her what kind of spaghetti sauce she used and, get this – she made her own! My mouth is watering just thinking about last night's dinner.

Oh, but it gets even better. So, the shells were pasta and they were stuffed with this meat sauce mixture that Mrs. McClelland made. It was all covered with cheese. I got there almost right as they were getting ready to pull it out of the oven so I got to see it while it was still bubbling!

They had that and fresh bread!! I have never eaten bread fresh out of the oven before, but apparently, she makes that, too. I always thought that hot fresh bread must taste something like toast, but it doesn't! This was amazing! The crust – which I normally hate and cut off – was thin and crunchy and the inside was still hot. The bread melted in my mouth. She had whipped butter on the table that they made from the milk they got from their own cows. I didn't realize last night when we got here that there was a whole farm thing going on.

I don't think I have ever eaten quite so much at one time

before. By the time I was done, I was so tired I barely noticed the huge bedroom they gave me. Cadence and I are sharing the room called the Green Room. They have it decorated with several different shades of green (which is my favorite color). There are two beds, each with a green quilt, and heavy green drapes over the two sets of windows. One set looks out over the front yard and the pond. The other set of windows has a gorgeous view of the mountains. We each have four storage cabinets in the room. I can't imagine that I will ever need that much room for my clothing. There are also plants everywhere in the room! I have no idea what any of them are, but they are all really pretty. I want to try to learn about them.

I want to write down everything!! The McClellands seem really nice. They told me they want me to feel at home. Oh! Last night before we ate dinner, they actually said the blessing. For a second there, I felt like I was on an episode of Little House on the Prairie – Mrs. McClelland kinda looks like Ma from the show. She's definitely just as nice and loving. I want this to work so much, but I don't want to be disappointed when it doesn't. I somehow always manage to find a way to mess things up. I wish there were a way I could talk to Jane and tell her how I'm feeling so she could help me sort some of this out.

It sounds like people are starting to wake up. I'm getting hungry. I can't wait to see what's for breakfast!

—

Today is Thursday, and the rest of the kids are going to school.

I haven't been enrolled yet, so the plan is for me to stay home until Monday. I am curious about the rest of the kids and really want to ask questions, but I am afraid to try to get to know them. Cadence is really quiet, which is a quality I like in a roommate. I think we'll get along well. Chloe and Zoe talked all through breakfast. I really like that the entire family sits together to eat meals. Even though we aren't really a family yet, it feels nice to be able to pretend to be a part of all of them. Chloe and Zoe are ten. Zoe told me at breakfast that they always have a hard time getting placed because they come as a package deal. They said there was one placement where they were separated. It obviously didn't work well. The two of them coming as a package deal doesn't seem to be a problem here. It feels like they take everyone!

It's too early for everyone to share their stories of how they came to be in foster care, but the stories are almost always the same. Abusive, drug filled home with lots of neglect or abandonment. Kids like us can be a lot, and most of the time we work really hard at making it difficult for people to like us. It doesn't hurt as much that way when we are rejected, or when yet another family decides we aren't worth the effort. Seriously, though most of us expect the adults in our lives fail us, so we push, and push hard to force their hand. Then when they do decide that we are too much to handle, we can say, "See, they gave up on me, too."

Brian came over to me and grabbed my hand again this morning. Cadence told me at one point that he doesn't speak.

He can hear and he used to speak, but he doesn't speak now. Cadence said she thinks he took a bad beating when he was three and hasn't spoken a word since. He's such a cute kid and so sweet, I can't imagine anyone hitting him ever.

—

After everyone else left for school, I followed Mrs. McClelland around the farm while she did her chores. I got to meet all the different animals. They have three cows, well, two cows and a calf. The baby is so cute! They also have goats, two horses, and chickens. It's funny to watch the goats run around butting things with their heads! There are a couple of cats around. Mrs. McClelland said that sometimes they come into the house, but they don't like to stay for very long, especially when Brian and the twins are around. My favorite animal is their dog, Koda. He's a big black lab who is so very lovable.

Mrs. McClelland said that he was crated last night when I came. She told me that whenever a new foster kid comes to the house, they put Koda in his kennel until they know how the kid will react to him. She said that a lot of times the new kids are really scared of him. He is a huge dog! I'll bet he weighs more than I do. He's really sweet, though and he stayed right next to me while we walked around the farm today. Mrs. McClelland told me the farm is just under forty acres.

She grows a lot of the food that they eat right here on the farm. In fact, almost all of the ingredients for last night's sauce came right out of the garden, even the herbs! She showed me this one area where she grows a whole bunch of herbs. It smelled so good! I have never seen fresh basil and oregano before. She started teaching me what the different plants are. There is stuff in the garden that I've never even heard of, like chives, tarragon, marjoram. And what the heck are lovage, sorrel, and savory? The one herb that she grows that I love is lavender! She let me cut a few sprigs and told me to put some in my pillowcase. It's good for calming people and helping them sleep.

She told me that we are coming to the end of the late growing season so she is trying to harvest as much as she can during the days so that the vegetables can be canned or frozen and the herbs can be dried. I'm excited because tomorrow she is going to teach me how to do some of the canning and how to prepare the herbs for drying.

At around noon we stopped and went in for lunch. Mrs. McClelland was reheating some of last night's leftovers. She told me that the red sauce is even better the second and third days because it's had time to really let the flavors meld together. While she was fixing lunch, she told me to go check out the library. It's actually the living room with a bookshelf that takes an entire wall! There have to be close to a thousand books on those shelves! There is another large bookshelf attached to a desk in the boys' room, but I won't go in there unless the boys are home and invite me in.

There are so many books! They have a little bit of everything. I picked out *To Kill a Mockingbird*. I've never read it before and I have heard so much about it. I curled up on the couch – both ends of the couch are recliners. The material is this really soft microsuede and it's so cushiony. As soon as I sat down, Koda jumped up next to me. I love that he is allowed on the sofa! I would hate for him to be scolded for snuggling with me. I grabbed the blanket that was on the back of the sofa and snuggled under it. Koda put his head on my lap and I started reading. I didn't get very far into the book before I fell asleep. Mrs. McClelland told me that when she came in to grab me for lunch, Koda and I were both asleep and looked so peaceful, she didn't have the heart to wake me. I slept straight through until the rest of the kids came home.

september 15

I did something stupid. Really stupid. I'm pretty sure I blew it, but it's not like it was going to last, anyway. Last night after everyone went to sleep, I snuck out. I grabbed some clothes, shoved them into my backpack and snuck downstairs. I looked around downstairs real quick to see if there was anything valuable looking that I could trade or sell. There was a ring holder in the kitchen next to the sink with a couple of gold looking rings. One of them had some diamonds. I swiped the rings, put them in my pocket and took off.

I know it was stupid, but I kept telling myself these people were too good to be true. They weren't going to keep me no matter how good I behaved so I should take off before I got too comfortable or they decided it was time for me to go. The last thing I need is to get attached to yet another family and have them yank the rug out from under me. I don't know that I could survive that again.

I ran away plenty when I was in Durham and Raleigh, but

it's a completely new experience out here. The noises at night are unlike any I have ever heard before, and they are so intense. The sky was totally dark and it was hard to see. There aren't any traffic lights or even cars moving around out here. I never realized just how many different shades of dark there could be to the night. I got out onto the road and was following the overhead electric lines. A very large shadow passed over me and I started to freak out a little bit. I looked up and saw an enormous owl had landed on the power lines. I stopped walking and just looked up at it. It had a white face which stood out in the darkness. I walked a few feet and I swear it tracked my every move, like I was its prey.

I got about halfway down the hill and stopped to look back. The owl was still watching me. It was so creepy. Its body was still facing the direction I had come from and only his head had moved. As I watched, I heard him hoot three times and he took off – heading straight for me!

He flapped his wings twice, his feet were tucked up under him and he flew right over my head. The feathers of one of his wings brushed across my face in a silent caress as he passed over my head. I could feel my heart beating in my throat! I started walking down the hill again. That was when I saw the eyes. At first it was just the eyes. It was as if a Cheshire cat were materializing out of thin air. I saw the pair of eyes glowing in the dark. It was only then that I realized the eyes were growling. I stopped moving. If I could have, I would have stopped breathing.

The eyes were about ten feet away from me. I blinked and one set of glowing eyes turned into four. And they all seemed to be creeping closer to me. I was looking around trying to figure out how to hide from these animals that I was pretty sure were about to rip me to shreds, when I saw headlights coming up the road fast! The growling stopped as the beasts that would have had me for dinner disappeared into the darkness.

The car screeched to a halt right in front of me. Right about the time I figured out the car was a sheriff's patrol car, the blue lights went on. Now I was a different kind of scared, but at least I was safe and in one piece. I can honestly say that I had never been that happy to be caught running away by a law enforcement officer.

The deputy got out of the car and asked, "Are you Storm?"

For just a brief moment the thought of running raced through my head. Chasing that thought was the thought of the creatures that the deputy had just scared away from me. If I ran away, I could be running right toward them – serving up their dinner. Instead of running, I nodded my head.

He told me to get into the patrol car and he drove me back up to the house. The whole five minute drive back to the house, I was silently preparing myself for packing the rest of my belongings as soon as we got there. He parked in the driveway and I could see that every light was on downstairs. I guess someone woke up and noticed I was gone.

He walked me up to the door where Mrs. McClelland was waiting. "Hey, Ann. I found this young lady on the road about to become coyote food. I thought you might want her returned to you."

"Thanks, Mitch," she said as she gave him a hug. "I'll take her from here."

I walked in absolutely terrified. I had no idea where I was going to be sent, and I really liked it here, but better not to get attached.

"Storm," she said. "Come sit down."

I was waiting for the yelling to start. Instead, she sat down next to me, gave me a hug and asked me if I was cold or hungry. Her calm was more terrifying to me than if she had been yelling. That I knew how to deal with. I always ignored it. But this was a whole new level for me. A wave a of fear crashed over me, making me feel cold from head to toe. As that fear hit, I felt like I could vomit.

Ann leaned back in her chair and studied my face. The way she was looking at me made me feel as though she could read my thoughts. She reached over and grasped my hand. "So where do you think we should go from here," she asked.

"I don't know. This is usually about the time that DSS is called and the group home/foster family says they can't deal with my shit and I get sent somewhere else." I was picking at my jeans and trying to act tough, like I didn't care what happened. Meanwhile, my emotions were all waging a war, trying to figure out which one would come out on top. Fear was winning.

"Okay. Yeah, I could do that. It would certainly make my life easier, not having to be up all hours of the night making sure you don't run away, but that wouldn't be a good solution for you. Maybe we can sit and talk about what happened tonight."

"Why aren't you yelling," I asked. I have never been brought back by police and not been yelled at.

"I could yell, but would that really solve anything? You wouldn't hear me any better, and it would just make my throat hurt."

By this point, I was very confused. She wasn't yelling, she didn't even seem all that upset.

She said to me, "What do you think we should do?"

I said, "I don't know. I've never had anyone act this calm after I ran away."

She asked me, "Are you planning on running again tonight? If so, I need some coffee."

"No," I said. "Those wolves out there were about to attack me."

She chuckled and said, "Those were coyotes. We don't have wolves around here. You look very tired. If you'd like, you can head on up to bed."

I told her, "I am tired. I think that going to bed is a good idea, but I still don't understand why you aren't mad."

She smiled and said, "I was worried, but not mad. I didn't want anything to happen to you. As soon as I heard the door open, I called Mitch and had him head this way in case you decided to take the road."

"You call the sheriff by his first name?"

"Mitch is not the sheriff, he's a deputy, and we have been

friends since we were little. Go to bed and we will talk more in the morning."

I turned and started to head upstairs when she stopped me again.

"Oh, Storm? Please put my rings back before you head up."

Without saying a word, I took the rings back to the ring holder and went up to bed.

—

After the rest of the kids left for school, I sat and waited. I kept waiting for her to say something - whether it was that I was getting ready to be kicked out, or that I was grounded. You've heard of butterflies in the stomach? Well, I felt like I'd swallowed a hive of hornets, I was so nervous. I ended up going to the kitchen to confront her. "So, what's happening," I demanded.

Mrs. M was sitting at the table, completely composed, sipping her coffee and reading a book. You would never know that she had been up half the night waiting for her runaway foster kid to be brought home by the police. She looked up at me in surprise and asked, "What are you talking about?"

I had so many different feelings swirling around in me and felt really confused, not to mention extremely terrified. "Why haven't you kicked me out? What are you going to do to me?"

"Storm, sweetheart, sit down." She patted the chair next to her. When I didn't move, she nudged the chair out with her foot and said a little more sternly, "Sit down."

I sat.

"Where were you headed last night?"

I shrugged and said, "I don't know."

"Okay, so when you got to you don't know where, what were you planning on doing for food, shelter, clothes?"

"I don't know."

"Sounds like a solid plan, kiddo."

I studied her face trying to figure out what her game was. I just knew she had to be mad at me. "I was going to sell the rings for money for food," I finally blurted out.

Mrs. M took a breath and said, "I kind of figured that. If you don't want to be here, you don't have to be. I am not here to be your jailer. I love kids. I love all the kids I've adopted and fostered. I would like you to give me a chance to love you. I think you could be a good kid, if given a chance. How do you feel about that?"

"Who are you?" I asked. "No one has ever talked to me like this. I was expecting you to take me back to the hospital and dump me just like everyone else has."

She took a deep breath and said, "Storm, when was the last time you felt safe in the home you were in?"

I opened my mouth to answer, then realized I couldn't. I don't remember ever feeling safe at home. I just sat and stared.

"You are not in trouble. I am not dumping you at the hospital. Even if I thought this placement wasn't going to work, I would never simply dump you. The way that I work is I take the time to talk to my kids. I want to know what you are thinking and feeling about being here and I want to share my feelings about how the placement is working.

"As far as I can tell, you have never had the chance to show what a good kid you can be. I want to give you the chance to be a good kid and know what it feels like to be loved and accepted for who you are. Will you work with me and help me do this for you?"

I hate crying. I especially hate crying in front of other people. By the time she was done talking, I had tears streaming down my face. I think for the first time in my life, it feels like there is an adult who truly cares about me. I'm not really sure how to deal with that. She told me that she wants to help me and when I start feeling anxious about being here, to let her know. I'm still not entirely sure what to make of her, but I've always been able to pick out fake people and liars, and I just don't get that feeling from her.

We were both quiet for a minute before she gave me a look and said, "I would like you to quit stealing my jewelry, though. If you need money, just ask." She winked at me and gave me a lopsided smile.

—

Mrs. M told me that today I am going to meet my new therapist. I only had two sessions with Jane, but I really liked her. I wasn't even thinking that I would have to start all over again with someone new. I know that it's required and that it's considered what's best for me, I just feel like such a loser. I mean, I keep failing at therapy. Okay, if I'm going to be totally honest, I usually feel like a loser at life.

Mrs. M must have noticed that I was really kind of anxious about the therapist appointment. She talked to me the whole way there and told me everything was going to be all right.

She told me, "Storm, just be yourself and be honest with the therapist. They are there to help you work through the pain and the trauma of your past."

I asked her, "How is someone who doesn't know me going to help me? I never know what to say or how to get started, I mean, do I start with being born addicted to meth and work my way to now, or work from now backwards? I don't trust new people and hate having to start over, but I am forced to start over all the time."

I startled myself by continuing and saying, "I don't want to have to go to yet another new home."

She was really sweet and she told me, "I don't want you to leave us, either. We are going to take this slowly, one step at a time, and we're going to do it together. Robert and I will help you any way we can as long as you want us to."

I could feel myself getting ready to cry again and had to turn and look out the window.

———

The therapy session went so much better than I thought it would. My new therapist's name is Caroline. She told me that she had spoken with Jane and wants me to continue writing in my journal. She said that she likes Jane's idea of doing daily writing prompts during the week.

Caroline is nice like Jane, but more new agey. I think if she had been around during the seventies, she would have been a hippy. I can picture her with the long hair, wearing bell bottoms with peace symbols all over her clothes.

Her office had lava lamps and bean bags. She had plants everywhere. I kept looking for a pot plant. As mellow as she acted, I'm pretty sure she smokes A LOT of weed when she isn't working. My favorite plant in her office was a lucky bamboo in a planter that looked like an elephant hugging the bamboo. There was also an essential oil diffuser on her desk. I think that she had lavender in it. As calm as I felt in her office, I had to wonder if she was diffusing a little more than just essential oils in that thing. Do they make Ativan for diffusers?

Caroline had all sorts of Asian stuff in her office. There was a chest that she told me in China would have been used for herbal medicines. Maybe that's where she kept the essential oils for the diffuser.

Caroline has this really cool mini Zen garden. It has miniature stones and sand and it even has a small rake so you can make designs in the sand. When I came in she had me pick up the Zen garden. She told me that she found people tend to relax and talk more when they are distracted. Maybe it's because when they are distracted they don't feel like their every move and expression is being watched. I know that as soon as I started playing with the rake, any question that Caroline asked me, I didn't think about as much and just answered.

Toward the end of our session, Caroline asked me if I knew yoga. I told her that Jane and I had worked on a couple of poses and that I had just started to look at videos right before my last grippy sock vacation. I said I really wasn't that good at it, but I wanted to learn. Everyone I see on the yoga videos looks like they are totally at peace.

She said she wanted to take me through a couple different poses and help me with some breathing exercises, then she wanted me to do some meditation. She made me start by closing my eyes and touching my fingers to the floor to "ground" myself. She talked to me about my breath and had me do some poses with her. She kept telling me that all the trauma that I have experienced so far in my life has all taken up residence in my muscles, organs and tissues. I don't know about all of that, but by the time we were done with all of the poses, I definitely felt calmer and more relaxed. She said that if I found myself starting to feel anxious, I could close my eyes and focus on my breathing. She told me it always helps her.

Right before I left she gave me the list of prompts for my journaling for next week.

september 16

I got to help make dinner last night! I told Mrs. M that I had never cooked before and she let me help. Everyone here has a job, even Brian. There is a chore wheel on the fridge so that no one is stuck with the same chores all the time. She is adding my name to the wheel today. Anyway, dinner last night. Mrs. M made homemade fried chicken. It was better than Bojangles! She said the secret is to marinate the chicken in buttermilk and hot sauce. She lets the chicken soak in what she calls her "super secret marinade" for at least a whole day.

She put a recipe in front of me for the salad. I always thought that salad was just iceberg lettuce and ranch dressing. This was nothing like that! There were three different kinds of lettuce, one was almost purple and kind of curly. One of the types of lettuce is called butter. It's a soft lettuce and I really liked it. Who knew there were different types of lettuce? Then there were other things in the salad like chopped up apples, and candied pecans. Even the dressing was homemade! I can't remember everything that was in it, but one thing that was really neat was Mrs. M has like fifteen different types of vinegar. I didn't know that there was anything other than just plain white vinegar. She has this stuff called champagne vinegar. That was one of the ingredients in the dressing. She had me run out to the herb garden and cut some sprigs of different herbs. Cadence came with me to show me the ones I didn't know.

Mr. M came home while we were all working in the kitchen. Erik was taking out the trash and the twins were setting the table. Mr. M walked into the kitchen, gave Mrs. M a hug and kiss and started asking each of us how our days went, if there was any homework. I had to wonder if this is what it's like being a part of a normal family. It certainly hasn't been a part of my experience with family life.

During dinner Mr. and Mrs. M did something new, at least to me. Everyone told me it's a dinner ritual that we don't do on the first few nights a new kid is there because it can be too overwhelming. They call it high/low. We go around the table and Mr. and Mrs. M ask what the high point of the day was and what the low point of the day was. Even after a couple of nights, it was still a bit overwhelming.

When they got to me, I froze. Mrs. M looked at me and smiled. I know she was trying to encourage me. Since I don't know anyone yet, I feel really awkward speaking in front of them. Everyone was looking at me so I jumped in, "There wasn't a low point of the day. Today I felt like I was a Disney princess. For me, the last two days have been the best days ever." Mrs. M got up from her spot at the table and rushed over to give me a big hug. She told me, "They have been really special for me, too."

———

Today was a really pretty day. Cadence, Erik and I went for a long walk. Behind the farm there is nothing but trees for what feels like miles and miles. Cadence told me that the farm is smack dab in the middle of Nantahala National Forest. There are trails all through the woods back there. We chose a trail and walked for hours.

Erik brought a map and compass with him and started showing me how to use them to map our way through the woods. He called the map a "topo" map and said that when you know how to read one, it can tell you all sorts of stuff about the terrain, like how steep it is, and different types of landmarks. He tried to teach me how to read it and how to use the compass to get my bearings and figure out how far away different points on the map were from where we were. He told me it was called land navigation. It sounded pretty cool, but I was a lot more interested in looking at everything in nature. I was happy that he was the one reading the map – we might not have made it back to the farm.

After dinner Cadence and I came up to our room and started talking about what I can expect when I finally get to go to school on Monday. She was telling me who the nice kids are and who I should stay away from.

Cadence is getting ready for bed now, so I am finishing up for the night. The last two days have been the best days of my entire life! I swear it feels like a dream. I have never lived anywhere so beautiful or had people around me who really seem to care as much as they do. It feels like I finally have a real family.

september 17

Today is Sunday. For the first time since I was taken away from my grandmother, I went to church. Mr. and Mrs. M said that they weren't going to force me to go. They leave it up to each of us as to whether we want to participate or not. Mrs. M said that religion and our relationship with God and Jesus is very personal to each of us and we should be allowed to "cultivate" (her word, not mine) that relationship however it is best for us. Erik and Cadence rarely go.

Brian and the twins came with us. Because Brian is only five, I don't think he gets much of a say whether he goes to church. He doesn't seem to mind it, though. The twins actually said they wanted to go. All three of them were dropped off in the kiddie classrooms before the start of the service. I think they do arts and crafts type of things that relate to Jesus and whatever the sermon topic is for the week.

It felt weird to be back in church after so many years. I kept watching for lightning because Grandma always told me I was evil, so stepping inside the church should bring about lightning and smiting. The atmosphere of this church was very different from Grandma's. I'm not sure how to describe it without sounding odd, but the whole place felt so positive. I got a happy vibe from being inside. The wooden pews were old, but shined like they had been polished. There was only one time during the service when I felt uncomfortable. There was a woman who walked by me wearing the same perfume that Grandma used to wear. When I smelled it, I felt my heart start to race. I broke out in a sweat and my whole body went ice cold. I could feel that I was breathing really hard, but I still felt like I couldn't get any air into my lungs. I looked all around because I just knew that Grandma was there and was going to make me go cut a switch. Mrs. M noticed that I was starting to breathe funny. Just about the time that I felt everything starting to go black, she put her hand on mine. I looked at her and she smiled at me. I closed my eyes and tried to breathe the way Caroline had shown me on Friday. I breathed in for a count of four, held it for a count of four, then breathed out for a count of four. I could feel it starting to work almost immediately!

I can't remember most of what was talked about in church today. Aside from the few moments when I really thought Grandma was there, it was good. I did end up finding out who was wearing the perfume. Mrs. M introduced me to the pastor's wife after the service ended and it turned out that she was the one wearing the perfume. I told Mrs. M on the way home what happened. She said she thought that maybe God's plan was for me to make a new, and good association with the perfume scent. I thought that was a bit of a stretch, but I didn't argue. I mean, who knows, she could be right.

—

I'm starting school tomorrow. I'm not sure how I feel about it. Everything has been so good since I got here. I want things to stay good. After church I watched a Disney movie with the twins. They love the original version of "The Parent Trap" so I sat and watched it with them. It didn't surprise me to find out that they were obsessed with a movie about twins! Brian came in and snuggled next to me. He is such a little sweety! He curled up next to me, I put my arm around him and he popped his thumb in his mouth. He was sound asleep by the end of the movie.

After dinner Cadence, Erik and I went for a walk around the farm. Koda tagged along with us. It's so funny to watch dogs. He sniffed at everything like it was the first time he had smelled it. When we got into the barn, he sniffed around outside of one stall, then went to the next. He stopped at a stall with what to me was an enormous horse. The horse bent her neck down as far as she could and Koda got up on his hind legs so the two of them could sniff each other and rub noses. She blew her lips at him and he got excited and ran around in circles. He ran out of the barn and came back with a carrot in his mouth.

Erik laughed and said, "Those two are best friends. I'm not sure if Koda thinks he's a horse or if he thinks Hornet's a dog.

You should see the two of them out in the field together. The funniest thing is when Koda gets on his back and starts wiggling around."

I asked, "Why is that funny?"

Erik said, "Because Hornet ends up on her back wiggling around, too. It's funny to look into the field and see a horse and dog both with their legs up in the air rolling around in the grass and dirt. And they do it side by side!" The image had all three of us laughing.

My mind wandered and I found myself thinking about going to school in the morning and I started to worry and feel anxious. My thoughts started to feel all jumbled in my head and I could feel my heart start to race. My hands were sweaty. My body had that shaky feeling that you get when you drink too many energy drinks all at once.

Cadence noticed that I had gotten really quiet and said, "Don't worry about school. I know it's going to be a new place, but you will go in with us. You will have two friendly faces there from the very start. My hope is that we have the same lunch period. It would be nice not to have to sit alone."

"I've kind of gotten used to sitting alone. I couldn't stand most of the kids in the group home and really didn't want to be near them at school. I'll be okay."

Cadence gave me a sad smile and said very softly, "It would be nice if I didn't have to sit alone anymore."

Erik said, "Because I'm a senior, I have a different lunch schedule. You and Cadence will probably have the same lunch slot since you're a freshman and she's a sophomore. We can all walk in together in the morning. Cadence and I can get you to the office for your schedule. Whenever there is a new kid in the house, either Mr. or Mrs. M comes with to make sure all of the paperwork is done. We'll make sure you get where you need to go."

"Why are y'all being so nice to me? You don't know me." I was really confused. This was such a new experience for me in foster care. And no one had ever been this nice to me in the group homes.

Cadence said, "All of us have come from really messed up families and we've all had turns at being alone and having to act tough or invisible when we don't want to. It's nice to be in a place where we can just be ourselves, act like a family and help each other. Even if we aren't really family. Mr. and Mrs. M work really hard to make sure that everyone who walks through the front door feels like they belong here. They are most likely going to push for adoption for you, if they can and if you want it."

I had no idea what to say. I couldn't remember a time when anyone cared about me. In one of the foster homes I lived in, the foster mom came right out and told me that the only reason I was there was for the monthly check I came with. She told me that she really didn't care what I did as long as I didn't cause trouble. I ran away so many times, I ended up in a group home. I'm pretty sure she was pretty pissed off until they placed the next kid with her.

By the time Mrs. M called us in to get ready for bed, the

three of us and Koda had been sitting out under the stars talking for hours. I knew more about these two people in one short evening than I had ever known about anyone. Even more important, I discovered that I liked them. For the first time in my life, I have friends! What is most important is that they are friends who could someday really be my family. The three of us walked back to the house together. Erik was in the middle with one arm slung casually around each of our shoulders.

It feels good to be a part of a family. Please, God, don't let me screw this up.

september 18

It's Monday. I am starting high school at Smoky Mountain High. I have been so nervous I have thrown up twice. I knew Cadence and Erik were going to be there, but I didn't know how I was going to do this. I hate having to start fresh in a new school. When I got down to the kitchen, Mrs. M looked at me and asked if I felt okay.

She came over to me, felt my forehead and said, "Sweetheart, you are white as a sheet. You aren't warm, but you look like you feel horrible."

Cadence said, "I think she looks a little green."

I took one look at the eggs on the table and sprinted to the bathroom.

"Storm." Mrs. M was knocking on the door. "Do you think you need to stay home today?"

When I finally finished my porcelain prayerfest, I opened the door and said, "No, I need to go. I'm just really nervous."

Because it was my first day, we weren't riding the bus. Mrs.

M took us in her car. She has an Expedition, so if we needed to, all eight of us could fit in it. This morning, she drove all six of us to school. Brian's booster seat fit perfectly in between the twins in the middle row. Cadence and I sat in the third row. Erik called shotgun and sat in the passenger seat. That was okay, because Cadence and I talked all the way to school. The twins got dropped off first.

We drove past the high school on the way to drop off Brian. Erik told me that on the rare days that Mrs. M takes us all to school, Brian is the last stop. The elementary school is tucked behind the high school. But, since today was my first day, the high school would be the last stop. When we stopped at the elementary school, Brian popped his seat belt off and turned around in the booster seat. When I looked at him, he gave me a big smile and a thumbs up.

I leaned forward and gave him a big hug. "Have a great day, little one!"

He grabbed his lunch box and backpack and jumped out of the car. Mrs. M made sure he got into the school and then we were off. The high school was literally two minutes from the elementary school. Once the truck was parked Mrs. M turned around and asked if I needed a few minutes before going in.

I closed my eyes and focused on my breathing, just like Caroline had taught me. I could feel my heart slow down and my muscles release. After almost five minutes, I opened my eyes. Mrs. M, Eric and Cadence were all looking at me.

"Okay, let's do this," I said with a lot more confidence than

I was really feeling.

The four of us walked to the front of the school together. Mrs. M was in front, Cadence and I were on either side of Eric. When we got inside the building, Eric gave me a big hug and told me to have a great first day. Cadence asked me if I wanted her to stick close to me and show me around. I asked her to stick around long enough for us to know whether we had the same lunch period. It turns out, we do!

After we figured out that we could have lunch together, Cadence went on to her homeroom class. Mrs. M and I sat in the office waiting for the principal to come out to meet me. We waited about ten minutes before his office door opened. He was nothing like I was expecting! I was expecting old and stuffy. Instead, Mr. Patrick was pretty athletic looking and energetic. He didn't really walk so much as bounce across the floor. If I had to make him into a Disney character, he would be Tigger.

He brought us into his office and gave me my schedule. There was another adult in the office – a woman he introduced as Ms. Weaver. She was the guidance counselor for the school. They talked to me about how to get around the school, gave me a map and helped me find my classes. They even showed me shortcuts that would help me. Just before they sent me on my way, Mr. Patrick said to me, "We are very happy to have you here at our school. I know you've had some really tough stuff to deal with, but I want you to feel welcome to come talk to me if you need anything."

Ms. Weaver said something similar. I don't remember now

what it was, but when she spoke to me, she had such a warm and real smile, I knew that she was speaking from the heart. Too many adults talk down to us and don't realize that we can read them – shoot, we can play them! It is so much easier for us kids to say something we don't mean and have adults believe us. They simply can't read us as well as we read them. I don't know, maybe it's just being bounced around in the foster care system. You have to learn quickly how to tell whether people are lying to you.

—

Today flew by! I was so tired by the time Mrs. M showed up to take us home that I fell asleep as soon as I got into the truck. The drive back to the house was only about fifteen minutes, but I felt like I had slept for hours. The only homework I had was reading a couple chapters from the book we're reading in English, *Animal Farm*. So far I'm really enjoying it.

My chore this week is to set and clear the table for breakfast and dinner. After dinner I got all the dishes rinsed off and into the dishwasher. Then I helped Mrs. M wipe down the table and all the countertops.

When I pulled out the broom to sweep the kitchen floor, Mrs. M stopped me. "Nope. Stop. You are not sweeping the floor. You've already taken care of all of the dishes. Thank you, so much for all of your help."

I asked, "Are you sure? It will only take me a few minutes."

She laughed and said, "Yes, go! The floors are Erik's job this week. Although I'm sure he would be ecstatic if you took care of them for him. He doesn't especially enjoy sweeping and it sometimes takes quite a bit of prodding to get him to do his chores."

After he finished sweeping, I spent the rest of the evening hanging out with Cadence and Erik.

september 19

After school today, I remembered that I forgot to do my journal prompt for Caroline yesterday. Her question of the day was: *What are the three things you like most about yourself?* Whew! That's a really hard question. There are a lot of days when I can't find one thing about me that I like. God knows, there are enough adults out there who can't find anything to like about me.

I ended up cheating a little so I could answer this. I asked Cadence what she liked about me. She told me that I was kind, funny, and really smart. I don't know if I agree with that. So I asked Erik what he liked about me. He looked at me and said, "Absolutely nothing." Then he started laughing. I slugged him in the arm and told him he was a jerk, but I had to laugh, too.

When I finished my chores after dinner, I went outside to sit on the porch. I had my journal with me and closed my eyes. I rocked in the porch swing (I have always wanted to live in a house with a porch swing - they are so cool!) and felt the breeze on my face.

Mr. M came outside and asked if he could join me. "You have such a look of peace on your face. It makes me happy to see you adjusting to all of the changes so well."

I opened my eyes and looked at him for a minute before speaking. "I like it here. It's peaceful. Y'all aren't doing this just for the check."

He started laughing. "Oh, sweetheart! Those checks aren't for us."

"Sure they are! Almost all of the homes I've been in the checks are like salary for the foster parents."

Mr. M got very serious. "Storm, we do get money for all of you. The state sends us a check every month for you. Ann and I decided a long time ago that the money we get from the state really belongs to you kids. We don't keep any of that money. It all goes into a trust fund for you."

I could feel my eyes starting to burn. I have always hated crying. I think it shows weakness, so when I start to feel that burn right before the tears come, I try to do anything I can to stop it. This time it didn't work. I could tell he was being honest. I don't know that I have ever met two better people! "How do you survive with six kids and only one income?"

"Wow, you are direct," he said. "The house and the farm have been in Ann's family for generations. She inherited all of this, along with a very healthy trust fund of her own when she turned twenty-one. Her family was pretty well off and my job pays pretty well, so we are fortunate that we are able to put your money aside for you for when you are an adult."

"What kind of job do you have?"

"I'm an ER doctor."

"Oh, why didn't the social worker introduce you as Dr. McClelland?"

"I'm not sure if she even knew. It's not a big deal. I usually introduce myself to my patients as Rob. I don't want to come across as stuffy."

I started giggling at the idea of Mr. M being stuffy. Quiet and kind, yes. Stuffy? Ha!!

"How did Mrs. M's family come into so much money?"

Mr. M tilted his head to the side and looked at me. "You certainly do ask a lot of questions."

I answered, "It's the only way you really get to know someone."

"How very true! Well, the story of Ann's family money goes back to the founding of the town of Sylva. On a cold night in January of 1879 there was a man, a drifter really, who walked into town with barely even the clothing on his back. He was cold, he was hungry, and he longed for a soft, clean bed to sleep in.

"He saw the flickering of the oil lamps in a house on the street. He approached the house and knocked at the door. When the door opened, there was a small man with a red mustache. The drifter stated that he was seeking lodging for the evening. It turned out that the man with the red mustache was named General Hampton. He was a local lawyer and the home the drifter had approached was that of General Hampton's father-in-law, Judge Cannon.

"Judge Cannon invited the drifter into his home where he fed him and offered him a warm, soft bed to sleep in for the night. The drifter introduced himself as William D. Sylva. Now, the judge owned some mills a couple of miles from the town and the next morning as he was leaving to visit his mills, he offered to bring Sylva with him and said that if he liked, Sylva could maybe work for him in his mills. It was honest work, he'd earn some money and the judge offered to have Sylva stay at his house until he decided where he wanted to settle down.

"The way the story goes, General Hampton wanted to build a town and knew that a railroad would be crucial for the town's survival. Sylva, who it turns out was loved by everyone, helped by working full-time at the lumber mill. He made sure that those saws were working day and night. The first building that was built was the general store. The second was the General's house. Finally, the General had a post office built. Now, he knew that he was going to need a town name for the post office. He asked his nine-year-old daughter what the town name should be.

"Mae, the General's daughter was so enchanted with Mr. Sylva that she said the town name should be Sylva. The General's wife agreed, and over Mr. Sylva's protests, the town name stood."

"That's a cool story. So Ann is related to Mr. Sylva?"

"Oh, no. Ann is kin to Judge Cannon. The family money

came from the mills and there were several lawyers. All of the money was passed down through the years. No one ever really knew where Sylva came from. He lived in the area for a couple of years. Interestingly enough, the second letter that came through the Sylva post office was addressed to him. It was postmarked Fort Gibson, Cherokee Nation. He pulled up stakes and blew out of here the same way he blew in – silently.

"No one knew where he went until 1951, when Jackson County had its centennial celebration. It turns out Mr. Sylva had moved on to a town called Cleburne, Texas. At some point he had a daughter. In 1951, she reached out to someone here in town to let them know that Mr. William Demetrius Sylva had passed away in 1927. Anyway, all of that history was just to show off that I know a little something about the town. Ann is related to the judge and the general – that is where her family money comes from."

We talked and swung a little longer before he went back inside. I told him I would be in in a bit, I wanted to swing a little longer.

I thought about what he had said about me adjusting well and realized that I have always adjusted quickly to new homes - I certainly have been in enough of them. I think that is one of the things I like best about me. I am able to adjust really quickly.

Honestly, as a foster kid, you really have to. I went to my first foster home right around the time I turned five. After six months, I was sent to another home. I still don't know if I did something wrong or if there was something wrong with the foster mom. After a while, some of the faces start to blur together.

Cadence told me I was funny. I've been thinking about that while I've been sitting out here. There has been so much ugly and negative in my life. I think me joking about it is how I deal with some of it. If I can make a really bad situation funny, it won't give me nightmares later. I mean, seriously, could I have survived Fangtasia if I couldn't find something funny about her?

There is only one place where I couldn't find the funny. I still have nightmares about it, but that's a story for another day.

The third thing I like best about me is that I love to read. Some people may not think that's such a big deal, but it's a way to live in another world. I wish I could teach more kids how great picking up a book and getting lost in it can be! I once read a book where the author described the woods so well, I could almost smell the peaty earth and the pine. I could imagine reaching out and feeling the odd, flaky, bumpy geometric texture of the pine tree's bark. When reading Little Women there were times when I felt like I was a part of the sisters' playacting.

I guess there are some things I like about me. Who knew?

september 20

Today's prompt was: *What do you need to feel safe?* I really have no idea how to answer that question. It's almost too hard. How do you ask a person who has never once in their life felt safe what they need to feel safe? Being here with the McClellands is probably the closest I have ever felt to "safe" but still not enough to completely relax. What if Mrs. M got pregnant tomorrow and decided that seven kids is too many? Last one in, first one out.

Do I think that's going to happen? No, but it's happened before. There was one family when I was about seven that seemed really great. The Wilkins. I had relaxed enough with them to let them in. I was really starting to trust them and feel like I could love them. Mrs. Wilkins was tiny and bubbly and always wanted to dress me in pretty dresses, and fix my hair and nails. There were a couple of days every month when she would close herself up in her room. I could hear her crying, and sometimes it sounded like she was getting sick or at least in a lot of pain. I asked

Mr. Wilkins once if she was okay. He said she was just really sad.

One day Mrs. Wilkins sat me down and said, "Storm, honey, I love you so much! You are just the best and sweetest little girl ever. Mr. Wilkins and I have always wanted a baby that we could love and take care of."

"I know, that's why you got me!" I was so stupid!

"Yes, honey. We wanted a baby more than anything in the world. And when I couldn't have one, we decided to adopt a little girl. We knew you needed a forever home so we brought you home to be our little girl. But yesterday I found out that I am going to have a baby of my own."

I was pretty excited about it. "Does that mean I get to help you with the baby? Can I be a big sister? I promise to be the best big sister ever! I will keep the baby safe and love it. I will even help with the diapers if you teach me how."

"Oh, honey." She sounded so sad, and I could see tears in her eyes. "We can't keep you and a baby. It would be too much."

"But, then, what are you going to do with the baby?"

"Storm, this is so hard for me. The baby will be mine for real. I want you to understand how much I love you."

I could feel what I used to call the fear and anger monster starting up. I knew that she was getting ready to tell me they were getting rid of me.

I screamed at her, "IF YOU GET RID OF ME, NO YOU DON'T LOVE ME!"

She burst into tears and covered her face. "I can't keep you both."

I rushed at her and started hitting her with my little fists. She curled herself in a ball to protect her belly, so all of my blows fell on her back and shoulders. I was in such a rage at that point I couldn't stop. Mr. Wilkins came in and pulled me off her and I turned my rage on him. They ended up calling the police on me. I kept hitting, kicking and biting at anyone who tried to stop me. Until they gave me a shot.

That was such a horrible day. I remember riding to the hospital in the back of the ambulance in restraints. There was a girl medic in the back who kept talking to me softly and brushing my hair out of my face. There was also a really huge, angry looking police officer.

When we got to the hospital, I heard the officer tell the nurse that I was basically feral and they should probably keep me in restraints. Apparently, I hit one of the officers so hard in the family jewels that there was concern as to whether he would be able to have children one day. The next day all my belongings were dropped off at the emergency room in two garbage bags. I never saw Mr. and Mrs. Wilkins again.

september 22

I was so upset after thinking back about the Wilkinses that I was very sick. I spent most of Wednesday night and yesterday throwing up. Every time that the memory popped back into my head, I was throwing up again. I didn't feel like writing anything yesterday. It was just too hard. I'm going to see Caroline today. Hopefully she isn't too mad about me not journaling yesterday.

—

My sessions going forward are all going to start the same way. Caroline is going to talk to Mrs. M about her opinion of how things have been going at home over the week. Then she will ask me. All of this happens with all three of us in the room. After my part is over, we will discuss any problems and what are reasonable steps to correct them. So far, neither Mrs. M nor I had any problems to report!

Caroline asked if she could see my journal entries for the

week. She said she really just wanted to see the ones that went with the journal prompts. I had to apologize. I had only done two this week. I told her I forgot all about the prompt on Monday. I was too traumatized after Wednesday's prompt to write anything on Thursday.

"Storm," she said, "the purpose of the journaling is not to traumatize you. However, with your background, it is possible that some of the prompts will bring up some very powerful emotions. Those are things I want us to talk about. You had a very powerful physical response to the stress your memories brought up. How are you feeling now?"

Mrs. M said, "Before she answers, would you look at what she wrote? I don't know if she wants me in here for this and I don't want her to feel like she has to speak in front of me. Storm, if you want me to leave, I will go. I promise you it will not hurt my feelings. We are here for you."

I thought about it for a second and said, "I want you to stay. This is part of why I am the way I am. I want you to know."

Caroline and Mrs. M read through the pages from Tuesday and Wednesday. Mrs. M had tears running down her face by the time she finished. She said, "I want you to know, number one, the chances of me ever having another baby are next to impossible now. Number two, even if I were to get pregnant, I would never give away any of you children! If you don't feel like the placement is working, come tell me. We will work on it together. But I will never put you out! And if you do decide you want to leave us, I will make you a deal."

"What's that," I asked.

She said, "I'll buy you luggage before you go."

I grinned at her. I was really starting to let down my defenses. I could really see myself growing to love this woman.

september 23

Last night after dinner was done and I was getting ready for bed, I kept feeling like I was forgetting something. Something very important that I needed to do, or something I needed to ask about. It was really bothering me.

I was brushing my teeth and repeating in my head, *What am I forgetting, what am I forgetting?* when I heard Cadence squeal and say, "OMG, you've got to come see this video of these baby goats! They are so cute!!"

The memory came back so fast and hard, that it literally felt like I got smacked in the head. In Caroline's office Mrs. M had said if she ever had "another baby." Another baby? She had kids that weren't fosters? I wanted to ask Cadence about it, but since no one had spoken about it, I didn't know if she even knew if there were other children. Mrs. M doesn't look old enough to have kids that are grown and gone. I'm almost afraid to ask her about it, because I don't know if it will hurt her or not. I guess I'll just play it by ear and if I find a good way to bring it up, then I'll ask.

I can't believe it's only been ten days since I got here. Ten days ago I was celebrating getting into my own clothing after ten days of feeling like I was being held prisoner in a room in the hospital. I keep finding myself letting down my guard with Mr. and Mrs. M. It has been so long since I have trusted anyone, but they really seem like good people. This whole family is amazing! I want to love them and be a part of them, but I am so scared I will lose them, too. I feel like everything important to me gets taken from me. I want to know what's wrong with me. Why am I so unlovable?

I mean, I see other kids at school who I feel are total assholes, but their families keep them. What is it about me that makes people want to throw me away?

———

Since today was Saturday and Mr. M was off, all eight of us piled into the truck and headed out for a hiking adventure - at what seemed like well before the crack of dawn! Mrs. M had a backpack ready for each of us. Each backpack had two bottles of water, some snacks and sandwiches, an emergency blanket, a headlamp (I was very confused by this one), and some wilderness first aid supplies. Apparently, these people take their hiking very seriously!

The park we went to was a really short ride from the house. I think we were there in about twenty minutes. The road we went down to get to the parking lot seemed never ending and then we just stopped in this gravel lot. Mr. M parked the truck and said, "Okay, everyone out!"

With all eight of us getting out of the truck at the same time, it felt kind of like one of those clown cars you see at the circus. Eric and Mr. M had a topo map on the hood of the truck and they were discussing elevations and different natural landmarks, and what the best approach should be. The twins weren't really complaining, but they really did not look like they were all that excited about doing this. Brian got as close to talking as he ever did and was hooting with excitement. He sounds like a little owl when he makes his hooting sounds. He was dressed like he was going on a safari - all in beige and with a little helmet, too. Cadence looked miserable.

I knew Cadence liked going on walks but I found out later that the last time they went hiking they hadn't done research on the trail they were taking. It turns out that Pinnacle Park (which is where they went last time) is a little over a seven-and-a-half-mile loop with a lot of uphill hiking. That hike took them over five hours to complete. Bonus - after the first mile, everyone but Chloe and Zoe took turns carrying Brian the rest of the way.

Today's hike was only about two miles out and back. The views were spectacular! We stopped when we reached the turn around point and Mrs. M spread out a blanket. We all sat and ate sandwiches. After I finished my sandwich, I stretched out in the grass and looked at the clouds. Eric and Cadence joined me when they were done. Erik pointed up at one of the clouds and said, "That one kind of looks like a wolf howling."

Chloe and Zoe joined us and started finding shapes in the clouds, too. We spent probably forty-five minutes pointing out the different clouds and what they looked like to us. I rolled over and looked back. Mr. and Mrs. M were sitting on the blanket watching us. They were holding hands and smiling. Brian was curled up on the blanket asleep. His hair looked like a bright copper penny in the sun.

The walk back took about thirty minutes, none of us were in a hurry, until we noticed that the sky was getting dark really fast.

Mr. M said, "It wasn't supposed to rain today, was it?"

Before anyone could answer there was a huge crash of thunder. We started to pick up the pace. Just as we reached the trailhead, the sky opened up! Rain was pouring down in sheets. Mr. M hit the unlock button on the remote and we all sprinted to the truck. Of course, we were all soaked by the time we got into the truck. Mrs. M told us there were small travel towels in our backpacks if we wanted to dry off. She really does think of everything.

september 24

Today after church everyone kind of scattered and went off in their own different directions. I grabbed *Animal Farm* and curled up in the living room with Koda. I have to write a paper on it when I'm done. Our teacher wants us to show how the book is an allegorical representation of the events leading up to the Russian revolution of 1917. I'm going to have to look up just about everything in that last sentence. I am enjoying the book, though. I find it interesting that the animals think things will be better when they take over, and they seem to be at first. But then things start to fall apart.

Mrs. M came in while I was reading.

We were alone in the house so I gathered up the courage to ask her about what she said on Friday. "Mrs. M, I want to ask you something, but I'm not really sure how."

"Storm, you can ask me anything. If you have to, just blurt it out."

"You said something in Caroline's office on Friday about

having had a baby. Did you have a baby?"

She looked so sad, and I wished right away I could have taken the question back.

"Yes," she said. "I had a baby about fifteen years ago. We had tried for a really long time and had actually quit trying because it wasn't working. I had been told that I had endometriosis and that children might not be possible. I was heartbroken, at first. Then I realized that we could foster and adopt so it didn't matter if I could have babies.

"In fact, Robert and I had already decided that even if we had children, we were going to continue to foster so that we could share our love, and some of our good fortune, with children who needed a home and love. We had already fostered several children when I found out I was pregnant. It was a very difficult pregnancy and I ended up on bedrest throughout most of it. When I went into labor there were a lot of things that went wrong all at once. The baby's heart rate dropped too low, I was bleeding. They ended up doing a C-section. The cord was wrapped around the baby's neck and she wasn't breathing. I was hemorrhaging.

"The doctor ended up doing a full hysterectomy. The baby had been deprived of oxygen for a long time, but they got her back. We named her Faith, because I had very strong faith that she was going to live. My OB came to me after Faith was born and told me that she had a condition called trisomy eighteen, or Edwards' Syndrome."

"What's that?"

"It's a genetic condition where there are three copies of chromosome eighteen instead of only two. It's also fatal. She lived in the NICU for twelve days."

I felt embarrassed that I had asked her about the baby after that.

She could tell I was uncomfortable. She said to me, "It's okay. I'm not upset that you asked. I loved, and still do love, Faith. She was very precious to me. I was hurt and angry when she died, but I prayed long and hard and realized that God does want me to have children. He just needed me to figure out that I was born to bring home the ones who really need me. You kids give me great purpose and I love it!"

She and I sat in the living room for several hours talking. I didn't share anything too deep, but I was starting to feel like I would be able to trust her if I did decide to talk about some of my past. She could have told me to mind my own business, or something even less polite, but she shared her pain with me. I think that means that she trusts me. I'm pretty sure she likes me, and that makes me happy.

September 25

Journal prompt for the day: *What do you worry about?* I think it would be a much smaller list if you asked me what I don't worry about. I worry a lot about where I will be tomorrow. Will I be in a home with nice caring people? Will I be in a hospital listening to the rantings of schizophrenics or the screaming of withdrawing addicts? Will I have food? Will I be raped or molested wherever I am? Will I be chained to a tree again and left outside overnight?

After the Wilkins abandoned me, I went to a new foster home. It was not a nice place. There were three of us kids in the home. The foster "mom" was named Candy. She kind of looked like what I feel a stripper named Candy should look. She had bleached blonde hair that was always teased and frizzy and makeup that looked like it was applied with a paintbrush. And everything she wore looked like it was at least a size too small. She was always wearing really tight short shorts and skintight T-shirts that showed off just a little too much cleavage. The only thing that would have been more perfect would have been if her last name were Cane. I don't remember her last name.

I do remember that the house was always a disaster unless social services was coming for a scheduled meeting. And then, the house got clean because us kids were told to clean up. It almost always smelled like a mix of stale sweat, pee, and cigarette smoke.

When I got dumped in Candy's lap, I was still so very angry. I had daily temper tantrums. I'm talking throwing myself on the floor, breaking things. I even hit and bit the other children. They always fought back. Had she been a little nicer, I might feel bad about some of it, but at that point, I felt like I was completely unlovable, so why should I behave? My own family didn't want me, so what did that say about me?

I think it might have been during my second week there that I had probably the worst temper tantrum of all time. Candy had made bean burritos for dinner. I didn't want a burrito. I'm not sure what I wanted, or if I even knew what I wanted. Honestly, I was most likely just being difficult. I told her I wouldn't eat the burrito. I could tell she was tired and not in the best mood. She said, "Whatever" and dismissed me.

That was all it took to send me into a rage. I picked up the burrito and threw it at her, then I launched the plate like it was a frisbee. It got a pretty good spin on it before it crashed into the wall. Candy was livid. She grabbed my wrist and hauled me out of my chair. I'm pretty sure that my feet were a couple inches off the ground for part of our trip. It felt like she had just about torn my shoulder out of the socket.

She took me outside and chained me to a tree. She screamed at me that if I was going to act like an animal, then I could stay in the yard like one. As she snapped the padlock shut on the chain, I noticed that there was a glob of refried bean right in the middle of her cleavage. I was chained to the tree all night.

It's amazing how cold it can feel outside at night when it's humid. It hadn't been a particularly cold day. From what I can remember, I wore jeans and a short sleeved t-shirt that day. But, after the sun went down, and the temperature started to dip, the moisture in the air made it feel really cold. I stood, chained to that tree for over eight hours. I can still feel the bark scraping at my face.

Candy unlocked the padlock and released me from the tree the next morning. She asked me if I was going to behave. I felt like I probably should. I really didn't want to be chained to the tree again. I was so tired that morning and my legs were so wobbly. All I wanted to crawl into bed and sleep. It's very difficult to get a restful sleep while chained to a tree, Every time I would start to doze off and my knees would buckle, either my arms or my face would suffer more scratches from the tree bark. I'm pretty sure that part of the tree was embedded in my skin by the time I was freed. Candy made me change clothes and go to school. I wasn't even allowed to take a bath.

That day at school the teacher noticed that I had a lot of scratches and bruises on my arms. I was pulled into the principal's office and asked about the bruising. I told him I play rough at home. He asked me about the scratches and I said that I had been climbing a tree. It wasn't that far from the truth. I just knew that they were getting ready to get social services involved again. I could end up someplace worse than with Candy.

The principal tried to tell me that it would be so much better for me if I told the truth. He said that they could help me. I really was terrified. It felt like every place I was taken to live was worse than the last.

These are just some of the things that I worry about.

—

Today was a good day, even though it was Monday. I feel like I am starting to find my niche at school. I love that I can have lunch with Cadence. She, Eric and I have gotten pretty close. We have made a habit of going out for a walk after dinner at night. Most of the time Koda comes with us. I love that dog so much!

I think he loves me, too. When I am home he follows me everywhere. He even gets up into bed with me. I asked Cadence if she minded him sleeping with me. She told me she didn't care, as long as he didn't hop up into her bed, she was fine with it. I don't think she's much of a dog person. That's okay - I am thrilled to have him all to myself!

September 26

Today was an absolutely horrible day! It started when my alarm clock didn't go off. Cadence always wakes up right away when her clock goes off. Then she goes for her shower and gets ready for the day. So, she didn't notice that I wasn't up. By the time I got going, I was so far behind that I didn't have a chance to eat breakfast. I almost missed the bus. Then I failed a pop quiz in English on *Animal Farm* even though I have been reading and taking notes in class. I already feel stupid half the time, but today just really made me feel like a moron.

In math, of course I'm in the most basic math because I can barely add one and one and come up with two. I was sent to the board to show my work on one of the homework problems from last night. And just my luck, I was assigned one of the problems that I had no idea how to do. So, I got to the board and just kind of stood there. The teacher was like, "Anytime you would like to get started, Ms. Rogers." I finally had to tell her that I really didn't understand the problem and how to find the solution. Half the class laughed at me.

When the bell rang, I picked up my books and sprinted out of the class and ran right into Jillian Lancaster. She is one of the most popular girls. She's smart, she's pretty. She's also a bitch! She pushed me and yelled, "Get off of me, you freak!" I fell, landing on my butt and my head hit the lockers. Jillian and her friends walked away laughing. I heard one of them say, "What a loser!"

This was my lunch period. I would sit with Cadence, things would be right with the world and I could go to the afternoon classes feeling a little better about myself. When I got to our table, I found Cadence with her head down on the table, sobbing.

"Cadence, what's wrong," I asked her.

She lifted her head. There was a red handprint on her left cheek. Her mascara was smudged and running in rivers down her face. I could feel my chest start to tighten and my cheeks got really hot. I asked her very quietly, "Who hit you?"

She sniffled, wiped the back of her hand under her nose and eyes. In a weak voice she said, "Jillian, but -"

I didn't hear anything else. I was so angry! I dropped my backpack onto the table and stormed off. I thought that this must be what it felt like when people say they saw red. Jillian is a senior, so she has a different lunch period than we do. It didn't matter, though. I knew she and Eric had class together during my lunch period. Right then he would be in biology. I got to the classroom and was still enraged. I charged in, went around the back of her chair, grabbed a handful of her hair and yanked her out of her chair onto the floor.

I was on top of her, punching her over and over before any-one in the classroom was able to move. At one point, I grabbed her head by her ears and was slamming it into the floor. I don't remember much of what happened over the next few minutes, but Eric told me in the principal's office that he pulled me off her. Apparently, I ended up head-butting him. It looks like I might have broken his nose. He is going to hate me. He kept asking me what happened, why I went after Jillian that way. I told him not to worry about it.

Mr. Patrick and Ms. Weaver both came out of his office and looked at me. All I could think was, *It's over now. It was great while it lasted, but I need to pack up when I get back to the house.*

They called me into the office and had me sit down. They told Eric to wait outside, that they had questions for him, too. Just as they were closing the office door, I saw Cadence come into the outer office where Eric was waiting.

Mr. Patrick sat down behind his desk and was quiet. He opened his mouth to say something a couple times and each time he quickly closed it. Ms. Weaver sat in the seat next to me. She turned toward me and pursed her lips like she was about to ask me a question, but couldn't. She closed her eyes, took a deep breath and slumped back in her chair, looking very defeated.

"Storm," Mr. Patrick finally managed. He appeared to be struggling to maintain control of his anger. "I have never in my entire career witnessed such an astonishingly unprovoked act of violence. Can you please, tell me just what THE HELL

YOU WERE THINKING!!!" He had started talking to me in a rational, conversational tone, but by the time he got to the end of his sentence, he was screaming and had come out from behind his desk and was standing over me.

I thought for sure that he was going to hit me. His face was an unhealthy shade of red and I could see his left eye was twitching and there was a vein in his forehead that was pulsing. He was breathing so hard that his nostrils were flaring.

Ms. Weaver had been trying to get him to lower his voice. She finally stood up and put both of her hands on his chest and physically moved him back behind his desk. Ms. Weaver had him sit down and she perched herself on the corner of his desk.

"Storm," she said calmly. "Can you explain what happened this afternoon? We would like to understand."

I took a deep breath. I was struggling against tears. Just as I was getting ready to tell them what happened, two police officers and a medic walked into the office. I shot out of the chair and ran to the corner furthest away from them. I felt like a caged animal.

Mr. Patrick said, "Storm, you are going to have to go with them for an evaluation. Your actions today, well, we cannot tolerate that level of violence in this school."

I barely registered what he was saying as I watched the officers advance on me. All I could think about was how to get away from them. I needed to be able to run away, but I couldn't see a way out. There was no way I was getting around the officers. The two of them together looked like a frickin wall! They slowly walked toward me telling me to be calm. I lost it.

As soon as the one put his hands on me, I started fighting. One of them grabbed me so that my arms were cinched under his. He had me pulled in close so I couldn't move my upper body. It felt like I was being held in place by steel bands. I started kicking my feet and the other officer yelled at me to stop fighting. I never even noticed the medic coming up on my side. The officer who was yelling at me started walking toward me. I pulled up both of my legs and kicked them out at him. I connected with his chest and knocked him into the wall. The second I kicked him, I felt the pinch of a needle and the burn of something being injected into my arm.

I threw my head back trying to hurt the officer who was holding me. I started to feel the room closing in on me. Everything was going black and I felt like I couldn't breathe. Before I knew it, I was strapped onto a gurney in four-point restraints. As they wheeled me out of the office toward the ambulance, I could see Eric looking very pale and upset. He still had blood caked under his nose, which now looked crooked and swollen. Cadence was standing with him with red rimmed eyes and nose and tears still streaming down her face. What broke my heart was seeing Mrs. M standing behind them with her arms around them and tears streaking down her face, too.

—

After they drugged me I slept for a couple hours. When I woke up I was in the hospital, out of restraints. It took me a second to realize that I was no longer wearing my clothes. The nurses and techs must have stripped me while I was asleep, because I was now wearing hospital scrubs. There was a sitter at my door and all I could think was, *Here we go again.*

Mrs. M was curled up in a recliner in the room with me. I watched her sleep for a few minutes thinking how peaceful she looked, and how sad I was going to be to have to leave them.

A nurse popped her head in the room and said, "Hey, sweetie! I'm Emily, I'm one of the nurses here. Can I get you anything?"

I told her no. Then she said, "I'm going to be right back. I have some questions for you."

I curled myself into a ball and started to cry as silently as I could. I had no idea how badly I'd hurt Jillian (truth be told, I really didn't care) but I was terrified that I had just screwed up what had started to be a really great situation.

Emily returned with some cream cheese and chive crackers and a cup of soda. She handed them to me and then asked, "Have you ever been here before?"

"No, but I've been in other hospital psych units."

"Okay, I'm not sure how they do things in the places you've been, but now that you're awake, the emergency room doctor is going to come in and talk to you and do his evaluation. Then a psychiatrist is going to talk to you. We will put together a plan of care after that. Do you have any questions?"

I told her, "No." I really didn't want to talk, and I wanted her to be quiet because I wanted Mrs. M to sleep.

Emily was different than a lot of the other nurses who had worked with me. She wasn't acting like she couldn't wait to get away from my room. Her tone was different when she talked to me. Just as I was thinking that I would talk to her, Mrs. M woke up.

"Storm," she said, "are you okay? What happened?"

I couldn't answer her. I just shook my head and put my face in the pillow. I knew I was disappointing her, but I just couldn't explain the rage that had taken over me. I mean, I could feel it coming on, but I don't know what I could have done to control it. She had come over to sit on the side of my bed and was brushing my hair away from my face. Mr. M came walking through my door wearing scrubs. I heard him thank my nurse using her name. That's when it struck me that he was an emergency room doctor and I was probably at his hospital. Shit! I really just wanted to curl up and die.

Emily asked both of them if they could step out into the hall and talk with her. I could hear the murmurs of their voices, but couldn't make out what they were saying.

The sitter chose that moment to start talking to me. "It's okay, dear. You're going to be okay. Do you want to watch TV? Would you like me to turn the TV on for you? What kinds of shows do you like to watch?"

"Please stop talking to me," I begged her. "I really just want to sleep."

But, she kept going, "Do you want anything? You know, if you talk about what's making you mad, it will help. It's not healthy to keep it all bottled up inside you. When you do that, that's what makes you explode and become violent. You don't want to be violent do you?"

"Please leave me alone."

She kept going on and on and on. I was at the point where I didn't care if I went into restraints again, I was getting ready to throw my pillow at her when Mrs. M stepped in.

"Excuse me. You may be trying to help, but I believe she has asked you twice now to leave her alone. She has had a hard enough day. She told you she would like to sleep. If you want to watch TV, please feel free to switch with one of the other sitters while the nurse and doctor are standing here so that none of us have to listen to you continue to badger my daughter."

Wait, what? Did Mrs. M just call me her daughter? No one had ever claimed me as theirs before. I felt an ache in the back of my throat and a tightening in my chest as the burning of tears hit the back of my eyes. After everything that had happened today, she still wanted me to be her daughter. So many emotions rushed through me that I felt lightheaded. She wasn't going to throw me away!

I never noticed the sitter leave.

september 27

I still can't believe she called me her daughter. Right before she left yesterday, Mrs. M told me that if I wanted, she would like to adopt me. If she does, I would never have to go to another family again. This would be it – forever! I feel like I woke up in a fairy tale!

—

This is total bullshit! Yesterday Mrs. M was talking to me about adoption and today I'm told that I won't be going back to the family. WTF is going on? I asked if I could have the phone so that I could call Mrs. M and was told that going forward I would only be allowed to contact my legal guardian. Seriously? The woman in Granville County who doesn't know anything about me except for what she can read in the file she has on me in her laptop. I repeat, this is total bullshit!!

I just want to go home. The nice nurse from yesterday, Emily, isn't here today. I have a different sitter today, too. Thank

God! That woman yesterday was a nightmare. She wouldn't shut up and I'm pretty sure that once Mrs. M left and the TV went on, I could have hung myself with my bedsheets and she wouldn't have noticed. I'm pretty sure her eyes never left the TV. If she had been back at my door today, I would have made sure the movie was something really awful.

But, since I'm only fourteen, if I put on something inappropriate, like a rate R movie, she would say I'm too young to watch it. That's happened to me before. The "adult" told me the horror movie I wanted to watch was way too intense for someone my age. I wanted to ask them if they had read any part of my history. Seriously? Too intense? Watching Michael Myers stalk and kill babysitters isn't nearly as scary as some of what I've lived through. I find most horror movies to be funny and unrealistic. I'm sure if I brought that up in a therapy session it would have the psychiatrist foaming at the mouth.

I woke up a while ago to loud voices right outside my door. I heard what sounded like Mr. M raising his voice. I've never actually heard him shouting, so I wasn't sure at first that it was him.

"Damnit, I want to see her!" I heard him shout.

"Doctor, we are under strict orders from her social worker that the only contact she is allowed is from her legal guardian, the social worker. I cannot let you in."

I went to the door and saw that it was blocked by a security guard. I tried to push around him and saw a glimpse of Mr. M. I shouted, "Mr. M! Get me out of here! I want to go home!"

The guard pushed me back into the room. He really shoved hard, too. I ended up falling. I could hear Mr. M yelling even louder. I got up and ran across the room, right into the security guard. He told me to step back.

"Why? What are you going to do? I want to see Mr. M!"

The guard said to me, "Sweetheart, I know you're upset…"

"Shut the fuck up," I shouted at him. "You are keeping me from my family! I want to go home!"

By this point, I knew that I was out of control, and I could hear a lot of shouting and commotion in the hallway. There was so much noise I felt crushed by it. The guard was trying to talk to me while I was screaming. I finally pushed things too far and punched the guard.

Within seconds I had what felt like twenty sets of hands lifting me off of the floor and carrying me to the bed. I was kicking my legs, trying to free them. It felt like I was being attacked. I felt like I couldn't catch my breath and realized that one of the guards was laying across my body. Their hands gripping my wrists and ankles were twisting and burning my skin. It felt like rope burn.

I felt my left arm get yanked up over my head. I'm surprised it's still attached to my body. I could hear ripping sounds and then felt them tightening something around my left wrist while they yanked my right arm down.

While they were working to tie me down, I kept fighting with all my energy until I heard one of the nurses yell, "Hold her down, I don't want to get stuck!"

One of the guards held my legs down by pushing down right above my knees. It hurt so bad I swear I thought he was breaking my legs. That's when I felt something stinging my left thigh. The sting started burning. Right after the burning started I felt a sting on my right thigh. I had no more fight left.

The guards got off me and I realized that I was strapped to the bed. My left arm was above my head and my right arm was hanging down by my side. I felt cool air on my legs. I lifted my head and saw that the stupid paper scrubs had torn during my struggle, so quite a bit of the lower half of my body was exposed. I felt so embarrassed. What made it even worse was the fact that the restraints that were on my ankles had my legs spread apart. I felt like my private parts were on display for the entire hospital to see. One of the nurses came in with a blanket and covered me. She started to talk to me, but I turned my head away. On top of all the rest of my humiliation, I really didn't feel like sharing that I was crying uncontrollably.

Thankfully, the medication kicked in almost immediately and I fell asleep soon after she covered me. I was told I slept for ten hours after getting the shots. Honestly, at this point, I wish I hadn't woken up. Ironically, that's one of the questions they ask all the time: Have you ever wished you were dead or that you could go to sleep and not wake up. Today my answer would definitely be, "Yes."

September 28

This morning a Psychiatric Mental Health Nurse Practitioner (try saying that three times fast) examined me and determined that I require inpatient treatment. Oh, joy! Apparently, I am suffering from severe depression. Well, duh! Everyone has jerked me around so badly all my life, what do I have to be happy about? Of course, this time I blew it. Because I got into a fight, I have been taken away from the one family that might have been a forever family for me. I don't know if I will ever get to see them again. Adding to my good luck, the nurse practitioner told me that there is a very good chance that I will be charged with aggravated assault because of how badly I beat Jillian.

One of the nurse aides brings me my breakfast. I don't know how long it's been sitting but it looks really nasty – a couple of tablespoons of cold hospital scrambled eggs (you just know those didn't come from a chicken), a shriveled up sausage link and congealed grits. I can guarantee that criminals get better food in jail. I threw away my breakfast tray without eating and asked my sitter to call my nurse for me.

The really nice, pretty nurse from two days ago is my nurse again. The one named Emily.

"Good morning, Storm," she says with a smile. "How are you feeling? Are you having any pain?"

I'm looking at her thinking that she has probably never had a bad day in her life. "No, not really. I mean, my wrists and ankles are a little sore and so are the spots where the needles jabbed me. I want to know when I'm going to go home."

Emily looked away from me for just a second, but it was enough. People don't seem to understand that we kids know when we're being played. We know when adults are lying or about to lie to us. And we know when we aren't getting the whole story. So, don't lie to us. Just be straight. If it's bad news, we'll deal with it. You might not always like how we deal with it, but we'll be okay.

"So, here's the thing," Emily started. "The nurse practitioner who spoke with you this morning feels that you need more time in the hospital so you are going to be going to an inpatient unit."

"Okay, for how long?"

"Storm, you've been down this road enough times that you know the length of your stay depends on how well you respond to treatment. I can't give you a specific length of time that you'll be in the hospital."

I knew this already, but I was hoping to get a different answer. "Am I going to stay here? Not like here in the emergency room, but like here at this hospital?"

Emily made a face and I knew what she was going to say before she said it. "No. Right now there aren't any inpatient beds available here, so we have sent referrals to hospitals around the state. The first hospital that accepts you as a patient is where we are going to send you."

"Why won't you let me see Mr. and Mrs. M?"

Emily put her hand on my arm and said, "Sweetheart, your legal guardian made that determination. We didn't have anything to do with that decision. If it were up to us, we would absolutely let you see them."

"I want to call her."

Emily jumped up and said, "Of course! I will grab the phone and the number for you."

Emily returned to my room with a cordless phone and a yellow sticky note with a phone number scrawled on it. She told me how to dial out then left the room to give me what little bit of privacy she could. It didn't make any difference – my call went directly to a voicemail box. And of course, the mailbox was full.

I put the phone down on the counter in my room. I knew that without being able to reach my legal guardian, I wouldn't be able to change anything when it came to visiting with Mr. and Mrs. M. There was so very little that I had control over at this point, so I decided to go to sleep. I crawled back into the hospital bed, pulled up my blanket and closed my eyes. Some time while I was sleeping, Emily came into the room, took the phone and turned out my lights.

———

At each shift when the nurses come in, they ask the same questions: "Are you in any pain, are you feeling like hurting yourself or anyone else, are you seeing or hearing things that aren't there?"

I screwed with the nightshift nurse's head earlier tonight. I know it was mean, but I don't like her much anyway. When she asked me if I was seeing or hearing things that weren't there I said. "Yes," and started describing the shadowman that was coming out of the wall behind her. I told her she should be very careful because he has been speaking to me, telling me he doesn't like her much.

She left my room pretty quickly, but sent the charge nurse in.

"Storm," she said sternly. "What do you think you're doing?"

"What do you mean," I asked as innocently as possible.

"We all know that you don't hallucinate. What are you trying to accomplish?"

"I'm sorry." I really wasn't but, I figured if I said it, she would leave me alone.

"Seriously," she said. I could tell she was frustrated with me. "Storm, what did you think was going to happen when you said that? You know, we have been trying to be nice to you. Yours is a really crappy situation and none of us agree with what is happening. But please, don't mess with my staff that way."

When she said that, I started to feel bad. What I did wasn't very nice. It's not the nurse's fault that I'm here. She didn't force me to beat Jillian to a pulp. And, there were no voices in my head forcing me to hurt her. I just lost my temper because she hurt someone I love. Now, I'll probably never see Cadence or Erik again.

I said again, "I'm sorry." This time, though, I actually meant it.

The charge nurse sat down with me and said, "You know the family of the girl you attacked talked to a lawyer and wanted to press charges against you."

I tried my best bored look and said, "So?"

"Storm, you really did some damage to her - and I don't just mean marking up her face. Although, she's going to have bruises for weeks. No, she has a really bad concussion from you slamming her head into the ground. Why did you go after her?"

I looked at her, pulled myself up in bed so I could sit a little taller and I said, "Have you ever been called a loser, or trash?"

She shook her head no.

"Well, that's what I have heard my entire life, especially by entitled little bitches like Jillian. She doesn't know my life or what I have had to struggle with. I couldn't do a math problem, so the whole class laughed at me. When the bell rang, I was trying to run away from the classroom where everyone was laughing at me and I accidentally ran into her. She called me a freak and shoved me so I fell and hit a locker.

"I went looking for Cadence, who I wish was my real sister.

Jillian has been bullying her, but Cadence doesn't complain. She doesn't stand up for herself or fight back. But she is always so kind and gentle, she makes the day brighter just by being there. It had been a really shitty day, and when I found Cadence, who I knew was going to help me feel better about everything that was wrong with that day, I found that she had been slapped across the face by Jillian.

"I still have no idea why Jillian hit her. I have no idea what happened or what was said. I just know that Jillian has been tormenting Cadence since the day she started at that school and no one has done anything about it. I didn't think, I just got mad. I went after Jillian, because no one goes after or hurts the people I love."

The charge nurse looked very thoughtful. After a few moments of silence she said, "Thank you for sharing that with me. I don't know how much of a difference it will make, but if you will allow me, I would like to share that with the police, your family and Jillian's."

I nodded in agreement. I didn't bother to add that I don't think they're going to be my family anymore.

September 29

Thanks to the nurse practitioner, I have to go inpatient. Apparently, my behavior is not normal. Of course, I can't stay here, either, because there aren't any available beds. When that happens, the hospital reaches out to all the other inpatient hospitals throughout the state. They keep sending requests until a hospital with an open bed agrees to take the patient. I am going to be going to a place called Oceanside Mental Health and Wellness in Wilmington. That's like six hours from here. I think that the chances of me ever coming back to Sylva and seeing the McClellands again is probably very slim. I asked to call my legal guardian. Her phone went to voicemail and again the mailbox is full. I've been calling for two days and every time I call it's the same thing. Do these social workers ever even check their voicemail?

The nurses are all being very kind to me, but I just want to go back to the farm and be with the McClellands. I never thought that it would hurt so much to miss people, but it does.

I miss Mr. and Mrs. M. They have been the best parents I have ever had. I actually felt like I belonged there. I love Cadence as if she were my real sister, and Chloe and Zoe. I miss little Brian snuggling up to me asking me to read to him. And I miss Erik. I miss sitting on the sofa with Koda. I never even got to say goodbye to him. He's going to think I left him and won't know why. It might be stupid, but I loved that dog more than anything else in this world. And I know he loved me.

I curled up in a ball because I could feel everything that has happened over the last few months just growing. There was an ache in my chest that felt like I was being crushed from the inside. I couldn't breathe and, in a way, I was glad. I was pretty sure I was about to die, and to be honest, I welcomed the peace death would bring.

Someone was talking to me, but it sounded like they were talking through water. I could hear voices, but I couldn't understand what they were saying. The nurse flipped me onto my back and I felt the head of the bed lift. I opened my eyes and saw several worried faces around the bed. One of the nurse aides grabbed my hand and was gently stroking it. I could barely feel her touch, but knowing that someone was trying to comfort me helped.

The dayshift charge nurse spoke to me softly. She spoke so calmly, I was surprised when her voice started to register clearly. I closed my eyes and tried to get my breathing under control. I heard her speaking softly:

"Storm, it's okay. Shh, just breathe. You are okay. Do you

want some medicine to help you with your anxiety?"

I nodded my head, yes. As much as I welcomed death a few moments ago, if there is a medicine that could take away this crushing feeling, I would gladly take it!

"Emily, will you go pull some hydroxyzine," I heard her ask. "Storm," she said when Emily left. "Have you ever had a panic attack before?"

"No," I said when I could finally find my voice. "Is that what this was? It really sucked! I thought I was dying."

"A lot of people mistake panic attacks for heart attacks because they can feel similar: crushing chest pain, hard time breathing, feeling of impending doom."

"That's how I felt." I really thought that I was dying for a moment there.

Emily came back into the room with a pill and some water. The charge nurse scanned my hospital band, then the medicine, then she handed me the medicine cup and some water. After I swallowed the pill, she wet a washcloth, wrung it out and came to sit at my bedside. She had me lay back and she wiped my face with the cool washcloth. Then she talked to me in her soft, soothing voice.

"Storm, I'm going to talk to Dr. McClelland later today. I know that you aren't allowed to see each other, but I can talk to him and let him know you're okay."

"Doesn't that violate some Hippocratic oath thing," I asked.

"Do you mean HIPAA? I guess, yeah, it does since technically he is not your legal guardian and I don't have permission from your legal guardian. However, he is the director of emergency services, so because of his position, he has to be kept informed of any change in patient status. Since you just experienced a major anxiety attack that required medication, it is my duty to inform him of the change in your status."

I looked at her with awe and admiration. "That was a whole lot of bullshit."

She grinned at me and said, "I'm glad you're starting to feel better."

I said to her, "You were a problem child when you were a teenager, weren't you?"

She looked at me for a minute then said, "Let's just say that I am well versed in the art of spinning a situation to suit my needs." She sat with me a for a while after I took the medication.

When I reached the point where I was pleasantly sleepy and starting to drift off, she arranged my blankets around me to make sure I was comfortable and she left - probably to go talk to Mr. M.

september 30

I am leaving today. None of the nurses or nurse aides that were working yesterday are here today. It's just as well. I don't know any of the staff's names and I don't want to get to know them. I wrote notes for Mr. and Mrs. M, Cadence, and Erik. I hope that once I leave, someone will take them to Mr. M. It would probably be better if they didn't and everyone just forgot about me, but I never got to say goodbye. That's one of the things about being a throwaway kid that really sucks. I don't ever get to say goodbye. With some of my placements, that wasn't a bad thing. I have been dumped in a lot of different places, but I never get to leave on my own terms, when I'm ready.

One of the nurse aides just brought me some clothing and told me it's time to get dressed. The sheriff's deputy is here to take me to Wilmington. Yay, more change.

———

Did I say it was a six hour drive to the hospital in Wilmington?

Let me correct that. The deputy drove about as fast as a sloth runs. Molasses moves faster in winter! It took over nine hours to get to the hospital! Nine frickin hours!! That may not seem all that awful, but it was nine hours IN HANDCUFFS!!!! In the backseat of a patrol car. That's right, handcuffs. Apparently, I am such a hardened and scary criminal that the deputy was too scared to drive with me in the backseat without being cuffed. And she put them on too tight. I'm pretty sure I have nerve damage in my wrist now. As she was putting them on me, she explained that it was departmental policy that anyone who rides in the backseat has to be in handcuffs. I've been through the IVC (involuntary commitment) process before and I can assure you it is not departmental policy. I know that it is the officer's decision whether to handcuff a *child* who is riding in the backseat.

We left Sylva right before ten this morning. It's now nine o'clock. When we got here, it took almost two hours for them to get me through the intake process and get me to my room. Thank God I don't have to share a room with anyone! They have allowed me to have a journal - not the one I brought with me, but one they have provided - along with a psych safe pencil.

What is a psych safe pencil, you ask? Imagine one of the pencils you get when you go to play Putt Putt golf. Now, imagine that pencil slightly skinnier and a whole lot bendier with no eraser and you have a psych safe (shank-less) pencil. These things are made specifically for inmates and patients on suicide watch.

The best thing I can say so far is that the food here is pretty good.

October 1

It's funny. Every place has its own set of rules, but after a while they all seem to run together. During intake last night they handed me a folder full of stuff. According to the intake nurse, it had all the information I would need to be successful during my stay here. I flipped through it and said there was a piece of information missing, my discharge date. Somehow, she didn't find that amusing. I thought it was hilarious!

This morning when I got up, I read through the materials. One of the papers is a daily schedule of events. There are groups that I am expected to attend throughout the day. Everyone is apparently assigned to a specific group. I will find out later today which ones I am in. They have the residents here broken into groups according to age and "cognitive ability." I guess that means that being fourteen and intellectually challenged would land me in a different group than fourteen and academically gifted. Although, how many academically gifted kids end up in a place like this?

The daily schedule lists meal times, outside times, and a variety of different types of therapies. It even maps out when we have free time to workout and shower. They have this thing here to help them force kids to behave. It's called CLIMB (child life improvement and management of behavior). There are different levels and ways of earning rewards, but the kid has to behave. And with each level there is a new contract that we have to fill out. I haven't seen this program before. I'm kind of interested to see how, or if it works.

Mealtime in the emergency room was horrible. The food was always cold! Even when it was warmed up for me, it never tasted quite right. Either that or there wasn't enough. I have been told that the meals here will all be buffet style, and as long as we are in our meal time slot, we can eat as much as we want. I'm hungry. I hope they call me soon for breakfast.

———

Breakfast was surprisingly good! It was buffet style and there was a lot! I couldn't believe it, there was a tray of French toast, another of scrambled eggs, a whole tray full of bacon, too. There was a table that had bagels and muffins with different jellies. I took a bowl full of fruit and a bagel with cream cheese. I sat at a table alone and watched the other kids. At this hospital, we range in age from five to seventeen, kind of like at Mrs. M's house, only I'm pretty sure no one here wants this to be their "forever" home. I'm also equally sure that there are way too many kids who age out of the system while in here.

The idea of aging out of the system while in a place like this scares me. I know I still have a couple of years, but what happens if on my eighteenth birthday I am still in one of these facilities? Will they just hand me my clothing and kick me out? Will they give me any money or provide services to help me find a place to live, food, or a job? Will I even learn any skills inside a place like this that would help me get a job? I am wondering about all of these things when a girl walks over and sits down next to me.

"It's smart to stick to the healthy stuff here," she said in a heavily accented voice. "Look around, amiga. So many of the kids come here and get fat. Not me. I got plans for when I leave. What's your name?"

"I'm Storm."

"Oh, like on X-Men? That's pretty cool your mom named you that."

"Actually, that's...never mind. What's your name?"

"My name is Josefina, but most people call me Fina." I love listening to her speak, especially the Spanish words. It makes her seem so much more exotic, although to be fair, she is already pretty exotic. She has skin the color of tea with cream. And her hair! It is down to her waist, thick, black and curly. It almost isn't fair to have to sit at the same table with her.

"So, dime, Storm, why are you here?"

"Dee may?"

"Si, yes, di me. It means tell me. I'm sorry, I sometimes go back and forth. Anyway, what did you do to get sent here?"

"I, um. I really don't want to talk about it. Things were going really good where I was and I really messed up."

"You thought you found a family that wanted to adopt you, huh?"

"Why are you here?"

"My parents don't want me."

"How come?"

Fina tilted her head to the side and said, "Mi amiga, if I'm going to tell you, you have to tell me why you are here."

"Okay. You go first."

Fina laughed and said, "Okay. So, I don't like the rules. I want to do what I want to do. Mi madre cleans houses and mi padre does construction work. They work, like all the time and they want me to work, too. I don't want to work. So I found a boyfriend who has money. He likes to spend it on me and sometimes he just gives it to me. Sometimes we party, and this last time we partied a little too hard."

As she's telling me this, I'm thinking that she's going to have to share more if she wants me to talk about losing everything I've just lost. I tell her, "That doesn't sound like enough to get you sent to a long term inpatient mental hospital."

She shrugged and said, "I overdosed."

"You overdosed? On what?"

"I don't know. Like I said, me and Angel were partying. Angel gave me some drugs that night that he said were, like, better than crack. He said this stuff would make me feel like nothing out there could ever be a problem again."

I was hooked. "So, did it make you feel great like that?"

She shrugged and said, "I don't remember."

"What?"

"Like I said, I overdosed."

"Okay?"

"Have you ever gotten high?"

"Well, yes, but not on purpose," I said, thinking back to when mom's boyfriend gave me the acid laced sweet-tart.

"How do you get high, but not on purpose?"

"I'll tell you, but I really want to hear what happened." I really was hanging on her every word.

"Okay, so everything else is stuff I was told, but I still don't remember. I remember taking something Angel handed me, then I took a hit off of his pipe. I was told that sometime after that, I passed out and he couldn't get me to wake up. He panicked and called 911. The ambulance people gave me a whole bunch of Narcan and said I threw up a bunch on the way to the hospital. By the time I got to the hospital, my heart had stopped, they were doing CPR and the ER docs had to intubate me so I could breathe. I was in the ICU for like two weeks after that. I was in a coma for the first week. They said they weren't sure if I was going to make it for a while there.

"Anyway, after they got me stable enough, they had this shrink come in and talk to me and ask me all these questions. They ended up sending me to this psych ward and after a couple days there, they sent me here because they think I was trying to kill myself."

"Were you trying to kill yourself?" I was genuinely interested. I couldn't imagine someone as gorgeous as this girl is, who has a family who appears to care about her, feeling bad enough about herself to want to kill herself.

"No, I don't think so."

"You don't think so?"

Fina scrunched up her face and said, "I really don't know what I was feeling that night. Angel is really hot and he had been my boyfriend for about a year. My parents hated him and kept telling me I was not allowed to see him."

"Why didn't they like him?"

"They thought he was too old for me and said that they thought he was either part of a gang or did something illegal to have the kind of money he did. They told me I could do so much better. I don't know."

I asked, "How old was he?"

Fina said, "He's twenty-one."

"How old are you?"

"I'm fourteen."

"Holy crap! You know that's illegal, right? He could be arrested."

"We weren't afraid of that. I wasn't going to turn him in, besides I loved him. Okay, you know why I'm here. What's your story? How did you get here - and how do you get high but not on purpose?"

I was getting ready to tell her that my story wasn't nearly as interesting as hers, I mean seriously, "I got into a fight" was the best I had. Nothing like I almost died taking drugs from my boyfriend. I also didn't know if I was ready to share my story about my mom and her boyfriend. Right before I started to tell her about the fight, a staff member came over to tell us breakfast was over and we were to return to our rooms until our next scheduled activity.

—

In reading the information they have given me, I have learned that the kids' portion of this hospital is broken up into different wings to try to keep us with "age-appropriate peers." Each wing can take up to twenty-four kids. That's ninety-six kids like me all in one place! That's crazy! What's even crazier is that I have been told this hospital is always full and there's usually a waitlist to get in. I was "lucky" they had a bed available when my referrals went out. Oh, boy do I feel special!

The north wing has the five through seven-year-olds, the east wing has the eight through eleven-year-olds, the south wing has the twelve through fourteen-year-olds - that's where I am, and the west wing has the fifteen through seventeen-year-olds. The different age groups are not allowed to interact during "structured" times.

My first activity after breakfast was group therapy. Like I said, my wing has twenty-four kids on it so they have to break us down into even smaller groups so that the group sizes are manageable. I think the groups probably vary day to day based on the staff members working. Today, my group had six kids in it; two other girls and three boys. Fina was one of the girls, so I went and sat next to her.

The staff member who was running the group was a Hispanic lady who looked like she should have been a Disney princess. She got us into the room and had us all take seats. It was weird, I was expecting to have wooden seats all in a circle, kind of like what you'd see in the movies when they are having group therapy. Anyway, the room is one of the lounges that we are allowed to use and it has three sofas, a couple of recliners and a couple of overstuffed chairs. There is a large, flatscreen TV on the wall behind a plexiglass screen. Fina told me that so many of the TVs have been broken by kids having meltdowns, that they started covering them.

"Good morning, everyone, for those of you who are new this morning, my name is Vivian. I am a therapist here at Oceanside. I am going to be one of the staff members coming around checking on you while you are here. I will also be leading some of your group therapy sessions. Some of you will be seeing me on a one-to-one basis. I'd like to go around the room and have everyone introduce themselves and tell us something about you." She looked at Fina and said, "Something new. It can't be something you've said before."

Fina just rolled her eyes.

Apparently, the newest person gets to go first, so she looked at me, looked down at her clipboard, scrunched up her face and said, "Pink -"

I quickly cut her off, "My name is Storm, and I am originally from a small town in Granville County named Shoofly."

I could see Vivian making a note on her clipboard. I was going to have to make sure that someone updated my record. I cannot let people here know that my real name is Pink-Envy.

"Thank you, Storm. Who's next?"

After all of the introductions, Vivian had us talk about feelings and how we knew what we were feeling; for instance, when we get mad, how does our body feel? Do we tense up, does our stomach hurt? I had to think about it, but when I get mad my face gets hot. I tense up, too, but my face gets really hot. We talked about what we can do to help bring those feelings under control when we start to recognize that we are having them.

Vivian asked me what I did the last time I got really angry.

"I beat the shit out of a girl at school," I said.

She gave me a look and said, "Okay, was that a good choice or not?"

"Well, I'm guessing that since I'm here and not back at the farm with Mr. and Mrs. M, it was a pretty crappy choice. But it felt good at the time."

A couple of the kids giggled at that.

I could see that Vivian was trying to keep her face neutral, but just for a second, I thought I saw the corner of her lips twitching toward a smile.

Vivian took a breath and said, "Close your eyes and imagine you are back in that space. Right before you start to hit the other girl, how do you feel physically? Can you remember if you felt hot, shaky, sweaty?"

I did what Vivian asked and closed my eyes. I try to remember exactly what I was feeling between the time I saw the angry handprint on Cadence's cheek and when I threw the first punch.

I tell Vivian, "My face feels hot. I feel like the muscles in my arms and around my neck and back are really tense." In fact, my muscles felt so tense while I was remembering, that I had to open my eyes and force myself to relax. I actually had to rub my neck and shoulders to relax my muscles.

Vivian smiled. "That's good! I like that you can recall those feelings! Even better, I like that once you identified those feelings, you immediately started to work on relaxing your muscles. We have about five minutes left together this morning and I want us all to do a relaxation exercise and some meditation."

A chorus of groans went up and Vivian put up her hands and told us all that this would help us to feel calmer. She plugged in something she later told me was an essential oil diffuser that had a calming oil blend. She had us all stand up and reach up, stretching as tall as we could. Take a deep breath in and then blow it out as we folded over at our waists and reached for the ground. We did that for a few more breaths, then she had us all lay down - recliners, sofas, or floor, it really didn't matter where. Then she did what she called a guided meditation.

She had us close our eyes and imagine that we were lying in the sun on the beach. We could hear the waves coming (I think she might have put on a sound machine with the sounds of waves at the beach). With the first wave, she said, feel the wave wash up over your feet up to your ankles. As the wave returns to the ocean, feel the stress leave, feel your muscles relax. She worked those waves all the way up our bodies. I didn't think it was going to work, but I swear, by the time she got done, I felt amazing! I felt really light and relaxed. I understand a little better now why all the people in the yoga and meditation videos always have those goofy smiles on their faces.

—

Today is Sunday, so the next hour of my schedule is devoted to church. This is the one thing on our schedules that is not mandatory. They told me when I got here that they can't force us to go to services, but that they offer several different denominations and encourage us to attend. I was told that it might even bring me some peace. I loved going to church with Mr. and Mrs. M. It didn't feel right to go to a service without them. I ended up going back to my room and doing yoga instead.

October 2

Today I think I am going to try to avoid Fina. She seems nice enough, but I don't really trust her. I think hanging out with her will probably only lead to trouble and I can find that easily enough on my own. Honestly, if I am able to, all I really want is to go back to live with Mr. and Mrs. M. I am scared, though, because I don't even know if they would take me back after what I did, but I know I have to find a way to behave so that if they won't take me, maybe I can find another nice family who will.

I know that's a longshot. I feel like I've gone through every decent foster family in North Carolina (and then some). I know I've burned most of the group home bridges, but I really don't care about that. I really hate living in group homes. The staff working in those homes are always underpaid and don't seem to care too much about the kids. Don't get me wrong, I know there are a few good group home people, I just haven't run into them.

Today is Monday and on Mondays we have equine therapy

in the afternoons. I am really looking forward to that! I miss Hornet and watching her play with Koda. They were so funny together! I wonder if we will be able to ride the horses here.

———

At breakfast this morning I was able to avoid Fina. When I got to the cafeteria, she was sitting with some of the other girls who have also been classified as "human trafficking" cases. They were all laughing and speaking Spanish with each other. I don't know a whole lot about human trafficking, but it seems to me like these girls aren't exactly being forced into the lifestyle. I've heard little bits and pieces here and there about them trying to find a way to run away. I need to stay away from that.

I got my breakfast tray and looked around. There was a table with one girl sitting by herself. I walked over and asked if I could sit with her. She answered me really quietly, almost in a whisper.

"Hey," I said. "I'm Storm."

She mumbled very quietly, "Hi, I'm Jessica."

Jessica seemed painfully shy. She had shoulder length strawberry blond hair that was very curly. Her skin was paper white. I felt like if she turned just the right way in the light, it might be possible to see through her skin. She had a huge reddish-purple birthmark that crept up through the collar of her shirt and covered about half of her neck. It looked like a really large bruise. She had really pretty green eyes with dark purple smudges under them, making it look like she rarely ever slept.

I said to her, "Hey, I'm new. Yesterday was my first full day here. How long have you been here?"

Jessica put down her paper spoon and said, "I've been here three months."

"That's a long time."

She cocked her head to the side and looked at me. "I saw you having breakfast with Fina yesterday. Do you really think it's a good idea to be seen eating with me?"

I made a face and said, "I'm sorry, but I just met her. I don't need her permission to eat with anyone. Hey, I'm going to run up and grab some napkins, do you want a real spoon?"

A blush crept up her face and she said, "I am not allowed regular utensils. I have made too many weapons out of them."

We ate in silence for a few minutes then I asked her what brought her here to the hospital. She told me that for the last few years she has been battling with depression. Every once in a while, her feelings would get so jumbled she couldn't tell what was happening inside her head. She said it was like all this excess pressure just building and building. She had no idea how to handle it or what to do with it. The first time it happened, she was ten. She said she felt like a balloon that had been blown up too much and she was about to pop. She was helping her mom wash the dishes and the solution came to her accidentally. She was washing one of the very sharp steak knives and it slipped in her hand. It sliced open her palm.

She said that when the knife cut her, the pain was horrible, but freeing. It felt like all of the pressure that had been building up was let go. She said she could almost see the pressure draining out of her with the blood that flowed from her hand. Her mom freaked out, wrapped a dish towel around her hand and took her to the emergency room for stitches.

She started cutting on a regular basis after that. I looked at her arms and said that she must heal really well because there weren't any scars. I have seen the arms of a lot of girls who cut. Many of them have scars that go from wrist to elbow, but Jessica's arms were smooth. That's when she lifted the hem of the skirt she was wearing and showed me her legs.

Her thighs were a mess! There were angry red welts and scars everywhere. There was scar tissue on top of scar tissue running from her knees to the tops of her thighs. And it wasn't just on the tops of the thighs, it was also on her inner and outer thighs. She was just pulling down the hem of her skirt when there was a loud crash coming from where Fina and her friends were sitting.

I looked over just in time to see a light skinned African American girl punch one of the girls at the table hard enough to knock her off her feet onto a pile of breakfast trays on the floor. The crash apparently came from the breakfast trays being swept off the table.

"You fucking bitch," the girl screamed. "Who the fuck do you think you are?" She picked up the girl on the floor by her shirt and punched her again.

After she threw the second punch, the other three girls at the table jumped up and started throwing punches. It was one against three, and the three human trafficking girls were losing. I mean, she even picked up one of the trays and smashed one of the girls in the face with it. The one who got hit first was on the ground. She wasn't moving. It didn't look like she was going to get back up anytime soon.

Jessica seemed glued to her seat, eyes wide and mouth hanging open. I was up and trying to drag her out of her seat so we would stay out of the fight. The girl who had started the fight was throwing some really powerful punches and it looked like all of them liked to fight dirty. This was not a fight I wanted to be involved with. I tugged on Jessica's arm, I was kind of scared I was going to pull it out of its socket, just as a wave of people in blue uniforms came rushing in and surrounded the fighting girls.

One of the staff members went around the cafeteria shouting that all of us needed to return to our rooms immediately, close our doors and wait for further instructions. At about that point, I heard a siren going off over the PA system. More staff members flooded into the cafeteria. Some of them were breaking up the fight, some of them were herding the rest of us back to safety.

So now, I'm back in my room. I'm not too worried about the possibility of missing group therapy or tutor time. I just hope that whatever that fight was all about doesn't keep me from equine therapy.

It took forty-five minutes for the staff to break up the fight. I've seen enough of these in hospitals that I know the girl who started the fight has been medicated and has to be in restraints. She was a big girl! I am pretty tough, and I've been in my fair share of fights. As many fights as I have been in, I have to say, I really hope I never have to square up against Big Bertha. Anyway, the two girls I saw who were hit the hardest were either moved to a medical unit, or quite possibly even to the emergency room of the local hospital. I'm pretty sure they both had concussions. I don't know if this hospital is able to deal with that kind of problem.

The other thing that happens after fights and patient meltdowns like this is the debrief. I once had a room right next to the area where the staff and security would have their debrief huddles, and I liked to listen in. I would sit on the floor next to my door and crack it open just enough to hear them. They never seemed to realize that the way the unit was designed, they could be whispering in their huddle and the sound still carried loud and clear to my door.

In their debrief, the charge nurse or head of security would ask what went well. What could have gone better. Was anyone injured? Did anyone want to press charges? I would have loved to have been able to hear this debrief. I'm also nosy enough, I want to know what started the fight and how badly Fina and her friends were hurt. The other girl didn't look like anyone had been able to touch her.

—

Equine therapy was so much fun! I am so excited! I found out that I will be able to ride the horse, eventually. I was told that before riding, I have to work my way up to that by taking care of the horses, the stalls, and the equipment. In the meantime, the horse and I need to get to know each other. The horse that I got is beautiful! The guy told us that the horses are all half draft horses who are used to working ranches and farms. They are used to kids sitting on them weirdly. And they are really patient. Like I said, mine is beautiful! She is black and white. Her face is all white except for this black star on her head. If she were a unicorn, that star would be where her horn should go. The rest of her body is black with patches of white that look like someone painted white swirls on her.

There is a guy who cares for the horses, they call him their handler. He told me my horse's name is Winona. I asked if that was like the actress Winona Ryder or the singer, Wynona Judd. He gave me a dirty look and said neither, that her name is Lakota for first-born daughter. I found out later that he is Lakota Sioux and is very protective of his horses.

The guy, handler, I really should ask him his name next week, made me start by mucking the stall. I had heard Mrs. M talk about it, and I knew it had something to do with cleaning, but I didn't know how important it is for the horse. So, first, I really didn't know that horses peed and pooped in their stalls.

I don't know why, maybe I was thinking that like dogs, they wouldn't want to sleep in their own ick. I guess they really don't have much of a choice - it's not like they can let themselves out of their stalls.

Anyway, if you leave the mess in the stalls, it can create skin problems for the horses. And, you know how bad pee smells when it's been around for a while? The guy was saying that the pee breaks down to ammonia and can damage the horses' lungs! So, we start learning about the horses by learning how to take care of them.

The guy told me that the first thing we do is take the horse out to the pasture/ring thing and let them run around. He said most of the horses are fine being in the stalls while we clean, but that we will be able to move around better if they are out. Besides, that way they get to run around and play. He told us that just like us kids, the horses need exercise or they start to act up. The image of a horse needing to go to time out made me giggle. I got a dirty look for that.

He directed me to a closet next to the tack room that had a bunch of tools hanging up. I was to grab a pitchfork, broom and bucket and bring them over in the wheelbarrow that was leaning against the wall.

After I had gathered all my supplies, he told me the first thing we take care of is the water. He showed me Winona's water bucket and had me dump the water, scrub the bucket clean and then refill it with fresh, cold water.

Then came the fun part: shoveling shit, literally!

We moved the wheelbarrow as close to the entrance of the stall as I could get it, I grabbed the pitchfork and the bucket and went after the big piles. He told me to pay attention to how many piles the horse had left behind and where they were. Kinda neat, he said they tend to use the bathroom in the same places over and over, like in a pattern. But, the important thing to note was any changes. If Winona left a bunch of piles today and then none tomorrow, she could be in big trouble! He also told me to pay attention to how her stall looks. He said today I wouldn't notice any difference from yesterday since it's the first time I'm working with her, but that her stall looks like it normally does.

Honestly, it didn't look that bad. He said that if I come back tomorrow and find that it's a huge mess, it could mean that she was in a lot of distress overnight - which could mean that she was sick. There are so many things that just the stall can tell you about the condition of the horse! After getting all the piles, he had me gather up all of the wet bedding. He said that we don't pull all of the bedding everyday - that would be a lot!

After we did all of that, he asked me to look around inside the stall to see if there were any hazards that could hurt Winona. Were there any nails sticking out, was the door loose?

After I had finished cleaning all the wet spots, we went for the bedding. He showed me how to spread the layers of hay and how much to use. He said that because the stalls had padded floors, we wouldn't need to use as much hay as if they were on cement. Once we had all of that done, he had me roll the wheelbarrow to the dump site and then let me go out to the pasture to bring Winona back. It didn't take as long as I thought it would. He did tell me that for the rest of the time I am here, Winona is my responsibility. So, I get to muck her stall twice a day every day!

If I ever get to go back home to Mr. and Mrs. M I will ask if I can take care of the horses.

October 3

This morning at breakfast I looked around and Fina and her friends weren't there. Jessica was sitting alone and waved at me. I went to sit with her and she asked if I had heard the news.

"What news?" I asked.

Her face was flushed with excitement. "All five of the girls who were in that fight yesterday are probably going to go to juvie!" She was breathless as she told me.

"Really?"

"Yeah, well, Fina and her friends are going to have to recover first. I heard that Fina got hit so hard, it broke a couple bones in her face. I'll bet she has a concussion or even worse! I wonder if that beating caused her brain damage." Jessica's eyes had a faraway look like she was envisioning the worst thing that could have happened.

I said, "I hope no one was hurt that bad. You said they're all going to juvie?"

Jessica pushed her eggs around her plate with her fork

and said, "Yeah. I hope they go. They have always been really mean to me. They make fun of me. One of them told me once that I should cut deeper and make sure I hit an artery. I over-heard one of the nurses say that one of the security guards got hurt pretty badly when they were trying to break things up. I couldn't hear what happened, but someone said something about emergency surgery. My guess is that they are going to be charged with assault."

Jessica continued talking about some of the mean things the other girls have done to her. I listen as she talks and I feel bad for her. These girls have really gone out of their way to break her down. Even with all of the horrible things they've said to her, she doesn't know how lucky she has been. They had been targeting her emotionally. As bullies, they were going to want her to suffer more than just the emotional scarring. It wouldn't have been too much longer before they started ganging up on her and actually hurting her.

Jessica was just finishing telling me a story about how Fina and her friends had made her give them her favorite stuffed animal, a stuffed sloth she'd named Bob, when I noticed Big Bertha walk into the cafeteria.

"I thought you said all the girls in the fight yesterday were going to juvie. Look who just walked in, Big Bertha."

Jessica turned to look. Her mouth dropped open and her eyes looked like they were about to bug out of her head. "No way! She doesn't look like she has a scratch or bruise on her, yet the other four are still at the hospital. Don't let her hear you call her that. She will kill you. Her name is Shiquita."

There was a little boy who looked to be about the size of a four-year-old trying to keep up with her. When he got close, he reached up and grabbed her hand. She stopped, looked down at him and smiled and the two of them joined the line together.

"Who is the little kid," I asked.

Jessica said, "That is Trevor. He is seven. He's been here for a little bit, too. He loses his shit all the time. When he does, he can scream for hours. It doesn't matter what the staff does to help him. Once he starts, he goes until he falls asleep."

"Are you sure he's seven? He looks like he's about four."

"Yeah, he's all sorts of messed up."

I was watching Trevor and Shiquita interacting in line. It looked like she was trying to help him. She seemed to really like him - she was smiling at him and being very patient. I was curious, "So why is he here?"

Jessica put down her fork and pulled her legs up cross legged onto the chair. She said, "He has such a sad story. His mom was, like, fourteen or fifteen when she got knocked up with him. She was running with a really rough gang and was on all kinds of drugs. He was born addicted to crack and meth, I think. Anyway, mom took off and left him with her parents. When he was about a year old, mom died, I think they said it was a meth overdose. Was it meth, or was it gang related? Anyway, it doesn't matter. His mom died.

"By the time he was five the grandparents were at their wits' end. They called social services for help and basically dropped him off. They said he would be better served in a foster home."

"They sent him to a foster home? That sucks!"

Jessica nodded and said, "I know, right? Instead of trying for therapy or something, they just dumped him. But it gets worse."

I scrunched up my face and said, "I'm not sure I want to hear worse."

She said, "So, his behavior got so bad that he was transferred from foster home to foster home. In two years he was in seven or eight different homes. He's so cute and small, that no one thinks he's going to be that big of a problem. Then he flips shit and is destructive and I think he even hurt one family's dog during one of his tantrums.

"Anyway, so he kept getting dumped on new families. The last family didn't even last a whole month. They got him and two weeks later called DSS and told them to come get him. They had packed up all his stuff - even gave him real suitcases so he wasn't carrying trash bags."

This is an exciting thing for a foster kid, we never have real suitcases, all of our stuff is hauled around in trash bags making us feel like garbage.

Jessica continued, "He was going to spend the weekend with a respite care family before he got placed in a new home. I heard his behavior was so bad, that there were three different respite care families in that one day. By the time they got to the third family, there had been so much confusion that his suitcases with all of his stuff had been forgotten somewhere. No one could figure out what happened to it.

"Again, he lost it! He started kicking the walls in the house and banging his head against the walls and the floor. He ran out of the house into the street and laid down in the street crying saying he just wanted a car to run over him and kill him. Can you imagine? They still haven't found his stuff, either."

I was shaking my head and thinking how horrible it was when a thought occurred to me. "How do you know all of this about him?"

She popped a grape into her mouth, grinned at me and said, "I have a room very close to the nurses' station. When I'm in there, I listen to every word they say. It's better than TV."

———

During therapy time I couldn't stop thinking about what Jessica had said about listening to the nurses talking about the different patients. I wondered if she knew my story. I wondered just how much of each of our stories the nurses knew. I mean, do they know about my mom's boyfriend helping me drop acid at four? Do they know how many foster and group homes I've been in? Do they know how many places have simply thrown me away?

I really didn't feel like talking during group. Vivian kept trying to get me to join in. I finally just said I didn't feel good and wanted to go back to my room. I was told to go to the nurse's station and let my nurse know that I felt bad. I told her that I was feeling really anxious and needed something to calm myself.

My nurse came with Zyprexa. They really make it easy to get medicine so that all you do is sleep. When I want to escape from reality, all I have to do is tell them I'm feeling anxious and they bring me Zyprexa. Once I take it, I turn out the lights, crawl under my blankets and sleep for about twenty hours. When I really feel the need to detach for a while, I act out. If I do something bad enough that they feel like they have to put me in restraints, I can get a shot of Thorazine, which is basically given to people having psychotic breaks. That knocks me out for two whole days.

I'm going to go take a nap.

October 4

I really hate this place. I want to go home. Does Mrs. M even know where I am? I'm going back to bed.

October 6

It might have been early morning when I heard whispering outside my room. I was having trouble opening my eyes, and I felt really cold but sweaty. I heard a soothing voice telling me to stay calm, and then there were a whole bunch of hands on me holding me down. Even my head is being held down while someone shoves something up my nose.

What did I do wrong? I can't remember fighting or getting upset. I felt a needle go into my arm and then a burning. I cried and heard more soothing sounds, but didn't understand anything being said to me. I felt a cool, wet cloth cleaning my face and neck. That felt nice. Then nothing but darkness.

October 9

I woke up this morning to something squeezing the crap out of my arm. I started to fight it until I looked and saw that I was attached to one of those hospital monitor things. I started looking around the room and was so confused. I had no idea where I was. Come to find out, I was in a real, medical hospital and had been for three days. My mind was blown when they told me it was Monday. The last time I wrote anything was Friday, but I don't remember writing.

It turns out that I had COVID. The last time I have any memory of writing anything was last Tuesday when Jessica was telling me about little Trevor. I am still hooked to an IV because I haven't had anything to eat or drink in several days. One of the nurses came in and told me that my nurse at the facility found me Friday morning with a really high fever and I was congested. They did one of those nose swabs and I had to come to the real hospital.

This morning I had this really cool nurse named Allison.

She walked in and I am not kidding, even with all of the extra space looking gear she had on, it seemed like the sun got brighter when she came in. She had this big smile and just seemed so happy. She brought me some JELL-O and started doing her exam. She asked me all sorts of questions and some of them seemed really silly. When she was done she asked me if I wanted her to come back and do my hair. I don't think anyone else other than Mrs. M has ever asked to help me with my hair.

It made me cry. Especially since, here she was stuck in the room with me while I'm sick. The benefit of me being in a regular hospital room is there are cabinets with hospital stuff. Allison went into one of the cabinets and pulled out this shampoo shower cap. I'm sure it has another real name, but that's what we were both calling it.

She put it on my head, got all my hair up into it, and started scrubbing my head. It was the coolest thing! It didn't need any soap or water added to it and it really washed my hair. When she was all done, my hair was wet and clean. She gently combed it out while I asked her all sorts of things. I started with why she wasn't wearing a mask.

She told me that she is wearing a PAPR which stands for powered air purifying system. The PAPR is this astronaut helmet looking thing. There is a belt that attaches to the nurse's waist with a battery pack. The battery pack connects a blower unit to the space helmet. The blower pulls air into a filter that blows into the helmet so the nurse can walk into a COVID patient's room without having to worry about getting it. Allison told me she prefers the PAPR to the N95 because she feels like she can breathe better. She told me that she is very claustrophobic and having the PAPR on makes her feel like she can breathe better. I told her that I thought that was funny. I would have thought that it would be the other way around.

Allison said, "A lot of people who don't know the different respirators tell me that. With the PAPR, I have a constant stream of fresh air and my face doesn't get hot and gross. When I have on the N95, I never feel like I can breathe. Then I start to get panicky. I have run into walls and almost knocked myself out wearing that thing. I will never do it again!"

I laughed at the image of her walking into a wall hard enough to almost knock herself out. Allison stayed in the room with me for a while longer. She made sure that I ate some JELL-O and drank a little bit of water. I asked if I could have something with some flavor. She brought me a cherry popsicle – I'm pretty sure it was the best thing I have ever tasted. After eating the JELL-O and popsicle, I was exhausted. Allison stayed with me until I fell asleep.

October 10

This morning they discharged me from the hospital and brought me back to the psych hospital. The medical hospital where I had been staying was in another town. We had to cross over a bridge to get back. It was kind of scary how high up the bridge was. It felt like there was a lot of wind getting ready to blow the van over the edge. I could smell the salty ocean air through the window that had been left slightly cracked open. The feeling of the sunshine on my face as we drove back was so very comforting. I asked, only half joking, if we could stop and go sit out on the beach somewhere for a bit before getting back. I promised I wouldn't try to run. I just wanted to be out in the fresh air and feel happy again.

My driver had the personality of a fence post. When I asked about stopping, she looked over her sunglasses at me in the rearview mirror and told me that we weren't stopping anywhere. She had express orders to get me back to Oceanside as soon as possible. Then she started ranting to herself in the front seat. She was making noises about not losing her job because some snot nosed entitled brat who didn't know how to act right was tired of being locked up in a hospital, when I should be locked up in a jail cell.

I didn't really feel like any of that was necessary, but it's a normal response with some of the people working in the behavioral hospitals. Don't get me wrong, I know that what I did was pretty bad. I still have no idea how badly I hurt Jillian. I know I am probably lucky that I wasn't just arrested and taken to juvie. Anyway, she seemed like a pretty miserable woman, so I rested my face against the window and looked at the ocean as we drove over the bridge.

I looked at the different boats gliding over the water. I really liked this one boat that was white and blue. It wasn't one of the little speedboats, but a huge sailboat. This one looked like what I would think a modern-day pirate ship would look like. It had two tall masts and I think I counted eight sails. It looked like it was moving pretty fast. I imagined what it would be like to be the one in control of that boat – steering it through the ocean water. I wondered if the crew of the boat got to see dolphins swimming alongside.

Just before the sailboat left my line of sight, I closed my eyes. Imagine how free it would feel to sail away on the ocean. I pictured myself setting the anchor somewhere in crystal clear blue water and diving off the side of the boat. I could imagine swimming in those waters for hours on end. I wondered what it would be like to be able to put on scuba gear and dive down to see the coral reefs. I conjured up a sea turtle in my imagination and watched the turtle swimming along in the muffled underwater silence. I was just imagining swimming alongside a shark when I felt the van jerk to a stop. I opened my eyes as I heard the driver say, "Hey, girl, we're here."

I know I shouldn't have said it, I know. And one day, I will learn to keep my mouth shut. As I exited the van I said, "You know, I do have a name."

She turned around real quick and slammed me against the van. Her arm had my entire upper body pinned to the van. I had been caught so completely off guard that I couldn't think. The wind had been knocked out of me so I didn't move. She said to me, "I know your name Pink-Envy. Named after a damn perfume. You better watch your step. I have no problem with taking you down. I know what you did to get yourself here. Your little punk ass shoulda done been gone to juvie a while ago."

I don't know what I did to her, but I am definitely going to try to keep my distance.

—

I could tell as soon as I walked into my room that someone had been in here and gone through my things. I don't have much in my room, but what's there is mine. I didn't think to hide my journal so I'm sure anyone who came through here read through it. I'm hoping it was just the staff and not one of the kids. I would hate for one of the girls from one of the gangs to have read through it. I really don't want anyone here to know that much about me.

The nurses checked me back in by having me strip out of my clothes. They told me they were checking me for contraband – like I really had an opportunity to pick up something while I was in and out of consciousness for the last week, but okay. They also told me that they needed to do a skin check to document any sores, bruises, or cuts that I might have on my body.

After they were done there was just enough time for me to go to dinner. I wasn't very hungry, but I wanted something hot to eat before showering and going to bed. I lucked out and was able to get a bowl of chicken noodle soup and asked if they would make me a grilled cheese sandwich. I sat at a table in a corner so I could keep my back to the wall and watch to see if anyone else came in. When I finished eating, I went back to my room and took a long hot shower. The psych techs round on us every fifteen minutes to make sure we haven't done anything to harm ourselves. The tech rounding on me came by three times before I finished up in the shower. I found a new pair of flannel pajamas in my clothing cubby, put them on and crawled into bed.

October 11

I made it to breakfast this morning with just enough time to grab a bagel and an apple. Vivian had left me a note saying she wanted to see me before group this morning. I got to her office just after nine. I knocked on her door and heard her call out to hold on for just a minute. I paced back and forth for a few minutes. The door opened and another kid shuffled out.

Vivian was behind her desk and called me in. "Hey, loca! I wanted to see how you were feeling before going into group this morning."

"Did you seriously just call me crazy?"

Vivian chuckled and said, "You know good and well I don't think you're crazy. I missed you. You had me very worried. I knew there was something wrong when you left group the other day. I just didn't realize you felt that bad."

"I'm okay. I'm really ready to go home. I don't want to be here anymore."

Vivian came around the desk, gave me a hug, and said,

"We're working on getting you out of here."

"I'm going back home?"

Vivian got that guarded look that all adults seem to share when they are getting ready to tell you something you really don't want to hear. "Where do you consider to be home?"

"Home for me is with Mr. and Mrs. M. They are the only people who have ever treated me like I belonged. I love them, and I know they wanted to adopt me. I have no idea how to get in touch with them, but they are home."

Vivian looked at the clock and said, "It's almost time for group. I would like to meet you back here after it's over so we can talk some more."

I felt pretty defeated because I was absolutely positive that she was going to tell me that I will never see the McClellands again. I told her, "Okay, I'll meet with you after group."

Vivian said, "Let's go."

As we walked to the day room Vivian asked me again how I was feeling and asked if I was still feeling run down. She suggested that over the next week, whenever I was tired to tell the staff and ask to be dismissed to my room. She said if anyone gave me any pushback to have them come see her. I figured she meant the psych techs. There are some pretty good techs here, but there are a couple who I feel like are just bullies. They don't seem to like their jobs, and don't even seem to like kids much. I'm pretty sure they are here because they need jobs but don't have any skills or education.

———

Today's group was probably the best one I have ever joined.

Vivian got us all in our circle and jumped right in. She said, "Over the past few weeks I have been with several of you during or after violent events. I have listened to you talking amongst yourselves and I have heard the word 'triggered' used a lot by many of you. Today I would like to talk about being triggered. What does that look like to you? What does it feel like? I am passing out paper and pencils so you can all take notes."

Shiquita asked, "Why? Why do we have to take notes? Are we being tested on this shit later?"

One thing I noticed about Vivian is that she doesn't react. So many of the kids do and say things that can be really outrageous and she keeps calm. She could be totally horrified or pissed off but her face doesn't give anything away.

Vivian answered, "No, Shiquita, no test. And if you don't want to take notes, that's fine. The notetaking is really more for you, anyway. If you feel what we are discussing could become valuable, it might be helpful if you take notes now so you can look at it later. I am hoping to stretch our triggering discussion over several groups."

There were several groans, and I have to admit, I was skeptical. All I could think was *Great, this is going to be pointless.* Everyone had started talking and the volume was getting louder and louder. Yet somehow, Vivian's voice carried over the noise as if she were using a megaphone.

"¡Escúchenme todos ustedes!" The room went silent. "Now that I have your attention, the reason this is going to take several sessions is because what I want to do is going to take several steps.

"First, we are going to define what being triggered means. Then we have to figure out what your triggering events are; could it be as simple as someone yelling; could it be a smell, or a particular person. What does getting triggered look like for you? Do you have an anxiety attack, do you get mad, are you going to react by biting yourself, hitting yourself or pulling out your hair? Another thing I want to look at is can you feel the changes in your body when you are getting triggered? The last part of this series is coping skills."

One of the kids, an older blonde boy said, "What if we have no coping skills?"

Vivian answered, "Most of you don't, and that is why most of you are here."

Shiquita said, "Damn, that was cold!"

Vivian responded, "No, I'm not trying to be cold. If someone in your lives had taught you how to deal with things that upset you, how to self-soothe, or even deal with frustration, the majority of you might not be here now. This is not something meant to shame any of you or make you feel bad. This is not your failing, but the failings of the adults in your lives up to now."

Shiquita said, "What if we were just born bad and there is no fixing us?"

"I don't believe there is such a thing as a child being born bad," Vivian responded. "I believe that life starts to mold us early on. If we don't like the shape that we see forming, we can change the outcome. Sometimes, depending on how far along in the molding process we are, we might need a little bit more help. Some of you have been molded a lot more than others, but I don't think any one of you is a lost cause. You were all brought to me for a reason and I intend to work with you and help you build and learn as many of the skills that I can teach you while you are still here with me."

It felt like her words knocked the wind out of me. I had spent so much of my life being told what a bad kid I was, I had never even thought to look at it from any other point of view. As far as I knew, the sky was blue and I was bad. I was stunned speechless, so I sat and watched as she pulled over an easel with one of those large pads of paper.

"What does it mean to be triggered," she asked.

All of a sudden, no one wanted to talk. Everyone was silent, I don't think any of us were even breathing.

"Come on, guys! Someone throw something out there."

A very tiny Asian girl who I'd never seen before raised her hand. When Vivian acknowledged her, she said, "It's an almost overwhelming emotional reaction. It happens because something has reminded you of a past trauma."

"Yes, thank you, Soonay, that was an almost textbook definition."

Vivian wrote the definition on the pad. Then turned around

and asked, "So, you said that getting triggered happens because you are reminded of a past trauma. What types of things can cause this?"

A girl named Nadia spoke up, "I get triggered when I want something and I can't have it. It makes me feel like I'm in a rage."

The blonde boy spoke up, "That's not getting triggered, that's called being entitled. It's because you're a spoiled brat."

"Blaine," Vivian cautioned. "Let's not start with name calling."

"What? I'm a rich kid, and I am spoiled. I get mad when I'm told no, too. That's entitlement, not being triggered. Triggered is when you smell the combination of stale sweat, cigarettes, and liquor that you smelled every time your dad came home drunk, smacked you around then raped your mom. Every time I smell that combination, or even parts of it, I feel like I need to throw up and hide."

Vivian nodded, and said, "That's a good example. Do you want to keep talking about it, Blaine? You don't have to if it's too much."

He had tears in his eyes, but he nodded his head. "My real dad would go out drinking when he would get paid. He wore this aftershave, and I can never remember the name of it, but it's part of the scent combination I always associate with him. When he would get his check, he would cash it and head straight to the bar. There was one place in particular that he really loved. He would drink, play pool and get really wasted.

When he would get home, if I was awake, he would hit me and yell at me for being up. The last night, I remember I was still in Kindergarten and I was drawing a picture for school for the next day. It wasn't late, maybe just after dinner, so six? I think my dad might have gotten fired from yet another job that day. He had trouble with work, but according to him it was never his fault. His boss didn't like him, the work wasn't what he had been told it would be. There was always an excuse, but it was never because of him. Anyway, he came home that night, took off his belt, grabbed me by the back of my neck and shoved my face into the sofa. Then he started hitting me with the belt.

"I was screaming, it hurt so bad. I still have scars from the belt on my back and the backs of my legs. My mom came running in and grabbed his hand with the belt. He let go of me, turned and punched her in the face. I can see the whole thing moving so slowly in my head. She fell backwards with her arms moving in circles. She was trying so hard to keep from falling, but she did. When she landed she looked dead for a minute.

"Dad walked over to her and pulled her up off the floor by her hair. She screamed for me to run, but I couldn't move. I watched him grab her, bend her over the back of the sofa and pull down her pants. That was when I got up and ran. I could hear her screaming and begging him to stop even after I was hidden in my closet and had my ears covered.

"When it got quiet I was afraid that my dad was going to come into my room and start beating me again. I stayed as quiet as I could. I ended up falling asleep in the closet. The next thing I knew, there were cops everywhere. One of them found me in the closet, picked me up and carried me from the house. I had no idea what was going on. Then I saw my mom in the back of one of the cars. I wanted to run to her, but the cop who was holding me said that I couldn't go to her, that they were going to take me somewhere safe."

I was watching Blaine while he was talking. His face was blank - there was no expression. Watching him tell the story was like watching him relive the movie of that night. He could probably see, hear, and smell everything that had happened that night. PTSD can be like that. When the memory has you in its grip the real world, the present moment slips away. The only reality is the memory that you have worked so hard to bury.

He continued, "I found out later that she was arrested after beating my dad in the head with a cast iron skillet. After he raped her, he told her to go make him dinner. She did. He passed out at the table while he was eating. I overheard one of my social workers one time saying that she hit him so hard and so many times there were pieces of brain everywhere and there was no way to reconstruct his face. She killed him."

Shiquita asked him, "Why was she arrested? Couldn't she just claim self-defense?"

Blaine looked over at Shiquita and said, "I think she probably could have, but she killed herself in jail. The official story was that it was an accidental overdose, but I'm pretty sure it was suicide."

When he finished, the tears streaming down his face, were

the only evidence to his emotions. His face was still an emotionless, blank mask.

Vivian said to him, "Thank you for sharing that Blaine. I know it couldn't have been easy."

He sat staring off into space and shook his head.

Vivian continued, "I would imagine that you have a very strong, and negative emotional response when you experience those smells. Do loud noises and yelling trigger you, also?"

Blaine nodded.

"Sometimes when a person is triggered, it can cause them to flash back on the event and feel like they are reliving it. Does that ever happen, Blaine?"

He nodded again, then excused himself and left group. Once he got out into the hallway I could hear him retching. There was a psych tech in the room with us and Vivian directed her to go check on Blaine.

Vivian looked at her watch then looked around the circle at all of us. "We still have a few minutes left," she said. "Does anyone else want to talk about triggers?"

Nadia spoke up, "I swear I really do get triggered by being told no."

"Nadia," Vivian began. "There is a huge difference between being triggered and having a temper tantrum. While both of those things involve strong emotions, and sometimes uncontrolled outbursts of anger, your temper tantrums because you have been told no are just that, temper tantrums. When they happen, your behavior and angry outbursts are an attempt to manipulate the situation so you can get what you want. It is not an emotional response to a past trauma. I know your last temper tantrum was over a toy that you wanted and weren't allowed to have. I can't imagine what traumatic event you suffered through over a Pokémon toy, unless one of the toys once attacked you."

By the time Vivian was done talking, we were all looking at Nadia, who shrunk in her chair. She looked completely embarrassed - and I'm glad. After hearing Blaine's story, I can't believe she tried to claim not getting a toy as a trigger. I really need to find Blaine later and see if I can find out more.

Vivian stood up and said, "I think that if no one else has anything to say, we are going to call it quits for today."

—

I knew Vivian wanted to talk to me, but I really wasn't sure if I wanted to hear what she had to say. It turns out I was right not to want to hear it. When she told me that they were working on getting me out of this looney bin, I had a feeling it was not going to be back to the McClellands.

I was right.

We went to her office and she had me sit down while she closed the door. That's when I knew there was a huge problem.

She walked to her desk and sat down. She took a deep breath then looked up at me. "Storm, I know your goal is to return to the McClellands. Right now, that is not possible."

"Why?" I know that they wanted to adopt me, bad behavior and all.

"Your legal guardian wants you to have a trial period with a local foster home."

"What do you mean?" I was confused. I thought things had been going well. "Why can't I go back to Mr. and Mrs. M? They told me they wanted to adopt me."

Vivian scrubbed her face with her hands, looked up at the ceiling and blew out a breath. "I want to send you back to the McClellands. I think they are a great family for you. My hands are tied because I have to abide by the wishes of your guardian."

I could feel the rage building inside me and knew that I was either going to start screaming or start crying soon. I said, "So, some social worker in Granville County who met me a couple times ten years ago is making decisions that she feels is in my best interests? How fucked up is that? She doesn't know me. She reads my file and decides that because I beat the shit out of a girl at school, who by the way hit my foster sister first, I can't stay with the only family who has ever loved me just for me? She doesn't even answer the phone when I call. I have tried calling her since the day I went to the hospital. All I ever get is a full voicemail box. How is that even fair?"

I was yelling at this point. I could feel every emotion I was feeling cutting at me - it was worse than any razorblade I could ever slice myself with. All of the pain was like a thousand emotional stab wounds. Tears were pouring down my face and I couldn't seem to slow them. The tears just added salt to what felt like raw, open emotional wounds. Then I realized I couldn't breathe. I was panicking. I could hear Vivian asking me what was wrong, but her voice sounded funny, like she was talking to me while my head was underwater. I saw her pick up her phone and shout something. She came around to me and crouched down. I don't remember falling to the floor. I could feel her cold hands on my face as she tried to get me to look at her. Her door crashed open, but I didn't care who was there, I just wanted to be able to breathe again.

I felt something sharp stab into my upper arm, then a burning sensation. All the while Vivian held my face and was talking at me. It didn't take long after they gave me the shot that I started to be able to focus on what Vivian was saying.

"Storm, it's okay, look at me. Breathe, Storm. Shh. It's okay. I've got you."

I closed my eyes and asked, "What did you just give me?"

The nurse, who was behind me, said, "I gave you Zyprexa. I was going to offer you a pill, but I felt like you were a little too far gone. I also didn't think you would have been able to swallow it."

She crouched down next to me, too and grabbed one of my hands. "I want to get your vitals in just a minute, but I want to make sure you're okay before I step out to grab the machine."

I nodded at her and she brushed my hair back out of my face. She smiled at me and left the room for the machine.

Vivian looked at me and said, "This has been one hell of a day."

I sniffled and said, "Yeah. And it's not even noon yet. Did this qualify as a triggering event? I'm just asking so you'll know

I was paying attention during group."

She looked at me in shock and started laughing. "Well it's good to see that you have kept that sarcastic wit! Storm, the placement is just temporary. I am going to fight for you to go back to the McClelland's home. You have to know this could take a while."

"I still don't understand how someone who doesn't even know me is allowed to make all of my life decisions. It isn't fair."

"No, you're right. It's not fair."

"So when I get to this new foster home and I do something they don't like, what are they going to do? Send me back to the hospital? What's that all about anyway? Whose bright idea was it to start sending kids who are acting out to the hospital? I've been to most of the ones in North Carolina and I can tell you, they don't do shit for therapy. All my life, all I have ever been is an inconvenience. Nobody has ever really wanted me, until Mr. and Mrs. M. Now I can't even see or talk to them. This new family, they're just going to throw me away like everyone else has my entire life. So what's the point?"

I could tell Vivian was struggling to find something to say that would help me feel better about the situation. In the end, the best thing she could do was sit on the floor with me, hold me and rock me while I allowed the Zyprexa to work its magic. I fell asleep on her office floor with her still holding and rocking me.

October 12

This morning I went to the stables for the first time since I got back from the non-mental hospital. The horse guy was there. He doesn't talk much unless it's about the horses. I like that about him. He watched while I guided Winona out of her stall to the paddock so she could stretch her legs and run. I had already gathered all of my supplies and got to work mucking out her stall. He didn't say a word while I worked, but he did grab another pitchfork and helped. We worked side by side in comfortable silence for close to twenty minutes.

After her stall was clean and all of the supplies put away, I walked over to the paddock and leaned on the railing, just watching Winona. She was rolling around in the dust. It was funny to watch her legs kicking up in the air. I hope someday I can find that level of contentment. I mean, not a care in the world, soaking up the sun and wriggling in the dirt. Okay, so the dirt part isn't great, but she seems to like it.

The guy came to stand next to me at the fence. He rested his arms on it and looked at me intently. He pointed to the horse and asked me, "Are you ready to learn to ride?"

I told him, "I'm going to be leaving soon for a temporary foster placement. It doesn't really make much sense to start learning to ride when I won't be here that much longer."

He nodded and said, "It's true you won't have the chance to learn to ride well, but we can get you up in a saddle today so you can ride Winona. You've helped to take care of her while you've been here, she likes you. You should have the chance to ride her."

"I'd like to try to ride her."

The guy went back to the tack room and returned with a pair of boots and a helmet. He said, "Put these on while I go get the saddle and the rest of the equipment."

He turned to head back.

"Wait," I shouted.

He stopped and turned around. "What?"

I asked him, "What is your name?"

He smiled and said, "Bear. I'll be back, Storm."

It surprised me that he already knew my name. He'd never asked for it or used it. He came back from getting the gear he needed for the horse so I could ride her. Once the saddle was in place and tightened, he told me to come to the fence. I climbed up while he brought Winona over. He directed me to swing my leg over and hold onto the reins. He showed me how to squeeze with my knees to direct her and kept talking about how to "find my seat."

Turns out, Bear pretty much grew up on the back of a horse and could ride a horse just like it was a part of him. He opened the gate of the paddock and guided us out to the pasture. He kept telling me to relax, that the horse knew what to do. He must have been able to see how scared I was. I felt like my whole body was shaking. Winona was a tall horse, and I had never ridden even a small pony. What if I fell off? What if she spooked? I've seen in the movies where a snake in the pasture can scare a horse and they throw the rider.

Bear rode next to me, speaking in soothing tones. I began to relax as I realized that Winona really did know what to do. I experimented with pulling on the reins, squeezing my knees and trying to guide her with my body. After two hours, Bear turned us around to head back to the stable. I know it's just a ride on the back of a horse, but I really feel like I conquered something out there today. My butt hurts now. Once we removed the gear from the horses, Bear showed me how to brush her down before she returned to her stall.

———

I pretty much skipped everything today. I know I'll probably get into trouble about it later, but I had no desire to join in for group stuff. I knew I wouldn't be able to concentrate on anything school related, so working with the tutor seemed stupid. The staff doesn't mind as much when you duck out of stuff on the weekend, but being Thursday, my lack of participation will probably cost me points on the CLIMB chart - whatever! I'm still only on the second of five levels and will most likely leave before I can reach the grand prize.

I took a shower when I got back in from my time with Winona. As I headed to the cafeteria to eat, I ran into Blaine. I asked if he wanted to go get some food with me.

He squinted at me and asked, "Do you really want to go eat with me, or do you just want to get more information out of me about what happened to me?"

I could feel my face turning red. "Well," I started. "I am interested in how you got here. You said that you're rich. How did that happen?" I know, my delivery was pretty blunt, but I couldn't figure out a better way to ask. I mean, it sounded like his real family was just as trashy as mine was and my family wasn't rich by any stretch of the imagination. The McClellands are rich, but I'm only their foster kid. That definitely doesn't make me rich.

Blaine looked like he was considering what to say. Then he took a breath. "I was adopted about a year after my mom killed my dad - me and my baby sister."

I gasped. "You never mentioned a sister when you shared your story."

Blaine said, "Yeah, she was about five months old when my parents died. My adoptive parents wanted a baby. Since we came as a package deal, they had to take me, but they weren't happy about it. They didn't like that I came with behavior problems because I had never seen anything other than violence and responded with violence when I got upset. No one ever taught me a better way to react. They have spent the last eleven years dumping me at hospital after hospital with a variety of different 'behavior problem' complaints."

"Were you really a problem child?"

"Yeah, probably. But it was always really obvious that they only wanted Joy. She had never been exposed to my dad. She was never beaten, never saw mom get beaten or raped. She was sweet, cute, and innocent. I don't blame them for wanting her instead of me. I'm just happy that Joy isn't afraid of me. She accepts me, ya know. At least she loves me for me."

"So what did you do that made them finally send you away the first time?"

Blaine's face turned red. He rubbed the back of his neck and looked at the floor. "I'm not proud of this at all. I will be sorry until the day I die. I always said I never wanted to be like my dad. One day my adoptive mom was picking at me. She wanted me to clean up my room, do this, do that. She just kept picking. She finally said it figures I'd turn out to be a lazy, worthless waste of air, just like my birth father.

"When she said that, I lost it. I already had anger issues, but I had never really lost my temper until then. I turned and I hit her - a lot. It was like all these feelings that I had kept hidden for so long all just came out at the same time. I told her I hated her and wished she were dead. Dad called the cops, and I was taken to the ER for an evaluation. I was only six.

"This place isn't too bad, though. And, hey, Miss Vivian really does try to teach us coping skills. Nobody else has ever done that for me. I mean, they always tell me *use your coping skills* whenever I lose my temper, but no one has ever told me what a coping skill is, how to work with it or how it can help me. Until now. Miss Vivian is the best therapist I've ever worked with."

I didn't know what to say to that so we walked the rest of the way to the cafeteria in silence.

October 13

After Blaine shared his story the other day, the rest of the kids have been opening up more. There have been so many stories that we haven't gotten around to how to deal with our "triggers" yet.

Today Theresa told us her story. She started, "My mama's name is Morganne. You might get to see her in here when she comes to visit every other month. She's really pretty. Anyway, Mama was twenty when I was born, and I already had three older brothers. Billy was six, Tucker was four and Hunter was two. I think I was a mistake."

Shiquita snorted and said, "Yeah, I'm sure the ones she had at fourteen and sixteen were well planned."

"Shiquita," Vivian cautioned. "This is not the time or place for judgements. Keep any comments that are not constructive to yourself."

Theresa continued, "Mama lived in government housing and had a neighbor named Lynette. Lynette was in her late thirties and had never been able to have kids. When Mama brought me home from the hospital, she asked Lynette if she would like to raise me. Mama knew how much she wanted a baby, especially a little girl.

"Lynette was so happy! Mama still came to see me every day, but Lynette was the one who was doing everything for me. Lynette's husband was a mean man and used to beat her. The police came to the apartment all the time. Whenever Lynette would call them, Mama would take me back over to her apartment. I remember he spent a lot of time in jail."

"The day I got taken away was a Sunday. Lynette wanted to make me look pretty for church. She had gotten this really pretty, frilly dress from Goodwill. She'd made this huge fuss about how it was such a beautiful dress and still had the original tags on it. She was so proud that she was able to buy me a designer dress.

"She put me in the tub and turned on the water. It started out really cold. She told me not to move, that she would be right back. The water kept getting higher and hotter. I remember calling to her that it was getting hot. Then I started crying because it was really hot and felt like it was burning. I started trying to pull my feet out of the water at one point because it was up over my ankles and it was burning really bad. I was screaming. It looked like the skin on my feet was starting to peel off.

"Lynette finally came back to the bathroom and saw me crying. She turned off the water and pulled me out of the tub. She called Mama and asked her to call the ambulance. We went into the kitchen and she rubbed butter all over my feet -"

"Why," Soonay interrupted her.

"Why what?"

"Why did Lynette rub butter on your feet?"

Theresa looked confused when she answered, "Because that's what you're supposed to do to stop the burn."

Soonay looked shocked. "You should never put butter on a burn! That only makes the burn worse and can cause really bad infections in the burn."

Vivian stepped in and said, "Soonay, you are correct. Butter is harmful for burns, but we can talk about that later. Let's let Theresa finish her story."

"Sorry, yes, please, continue."

Theresa continued, "The EMS people got to the apartment and my feet, ankles and calves were covered in blisters. They took me to the hospital, but I didn't stay at that one for long. I don't remember a whole lot about what happened in that first hospital, but I think my feet got wrapped up and another EMS took me to a different hospital. I was at the second hospital for a couple months. I had to have a bunch of surgeries where they took skin from my thighs to fix the skin on my feet. That's why the skin on my feet looks so weird."

Theresa was quiet for a minute then said, "You know, I don't remember Mama or Lynette coming to the second hospital even once while I was in there. The nurses were nice, though. They let me have JELL-O and fixed my hair."

Vivian asked quietly, "How old were you when that

happened?"

"Oh, it was right before my fourth birthday. I was supposed to have a Disney princess birthday party, but I guess Mama and Lynette forgot my birthday that year. Me being in the hospital must have been really hard on them."

I could hear Soonay mutter to herself that maybe Theresa wouldn't have been in the hospital if it hadn't been for them. In my head, I had to agree with her, but I don't think either one of us really wanted anyone to hear that particular thought.

Theresa is really sweet and thoughtful. I've seen her taking extra muffins from the cafeteria and sharing them with the younger kids when they complain they're hungry. I don't think she's very smart and I can see her sometimes struggling to come up with the right words when she's trying to talk in group and tell us how she feels. I have to wonder just how long Lynette left her in that scalding hot water for her skin to be peeling off of her feet. I also have to wonder how her "Mama" could just push her off on another person.

I mean, if you don't want to be a parent, don't have kids. To me this seems like a simple concept. I guess not, though, because I look around the room at the kids here with me in group therapy and have to wonder if any of us were wanted. On some level, we are all throwaway kids.

—

The rest of the day today was pretty much the same as every day - I saw the tutor, who told me my math skills still suck. I did my individual therapy with the specialist. I'm still not sure what that's all about, but I figure if I do what they tell me to do, maybe I'll actually be able to leave this place. I got to do some yoga today and pick out a new book. They have this rewards system here that they're all really proud of - I'm not sure why. You earn points for good behavior every day and get to trade in those points for stuff. I have to trade points for my books. I'd rather just have a library where I can check them out and return them when I'm done.

I guess the world would run a whole lot better if I were in charge - ha ha!

I saw that driver again today. She gave me the stinkeye and walked on. I still don't know what I did to offend her. Oh, well. I'm sure if I'm here long enough, I'll find out eventually. In the meantime, the kids around me have started to open up and share their pain. I'm not sure that I'm ready to - I really wouldn't even know where to start. There is so much about my life that I'm sure would be considered traumatic but for me, it's just the way it is.

I also have to wonder, is my pain really any worse than anyone else's? My mama didn't kill my dad. I never had to witness her being beaten or raped. I feel like all of the bad things that happened to her she did to herself. I don't know that for sure, but I don't think that anyone ever forced her to take the drugs that she loved so much. Grandma was a little heavy handed when it came to the switch...I don't know. Is being unlovable and unwanted considered traumatic?

I know I've said in the past that I would love to have a normal family. I know that the one I was born into is not normal, but what does normal really look like? I mean Mr. and Mrs. M aren't normal. Don't get me wrong, they are great people, but they definitely aren't normal. I'm not even sure how two people like them find each other. Both of them are willing to take in kids who aren't theirs, adopt them, raise them and give them a family. They don't even take the money the state offers. That's what really blows my mind.

October 14

If you've never been a guest in a mental hospital or behavioral health facility, you may not know some of the rules. One of the biggest is visitors cannot bring anything in when they come to visit. Today a visitor managed to sneak a small stuffed bear in for one of the girls who was here for drug problems and being suicidal. Apparently, there was more to the stuffie than just fluff. After the visit, she went back to her room and overdosed on the drugs that had been sewn into the bear.

The techs are required to round on all of us every fifteen minutes. I asked one of them why. Were they looking for something? What was the purpose behind checking on us that often? I thought he was being a smartass when he said that they are making sure we are all still alive - but that's exactly what they are looking for. He called it checking for signs of life. If we patients are asleep, they watch to make sure they can see our chests rise and fall at least twice before they move on to the next room.

I asked a nurse once why every fifteen minutes. She told me that if a person tries to hang themselves after a check, that brain function can still be preserved if they are found within fifteen minutes. I found that hard to believe. There are plenty of people walking around in here, both staff and patients, who haven't been without oxygen for fifteen minutes, and I'm pretty sure they're brain dead. I know, that wasn't very nice.

Anyway, the tech was doing the fifteen minute checks and stopped at her room. If the patient has their head covered, the tech has to uncover their head. I overheard the nurses say that when the tech got to her room, her blanket was up over her head. When he uncovered her head, her face and lips were blue and she was not breathing. I heard the overhead page for a code blue. There was commotion in the hallway, people running and yelling for a crash cart and portable oxygen and suction.

The rest of us were made to go back to our rooms. I wonder if they're going to start patting people down when they come in. There was a huge thing last week with Soonay's visitors. She has a therapist from outside who comes in daily. We aren't allowed to have outside food or drinks brought in, yet somehow, the therapist was bringing in these huge drinks - kinda like the Slurpees you get at the gas station. They can't bring in bags, purses, or anything else. How was she able to get this huge forty-two ounce plastic cup past security? Somehow no one noticed. When the nurses would go into Soonay's room, they would ask where the cups came from. The therapist was finally confronted and told that if she continued to bring in the food and drinks from outside the hospital, she wouldn't be allowed to come in.

She gave a little pushback and said that as her therapist, she couldn't be barred from visiting Soonay. I heard the charge nurse tell her that if she continued to break the rules, she would be allowed to visit Soonay only over a Zoom call. She said a huge reason behind their strict enforcement of these rules is to keep us kids safe – from the outside world and ourselves.

The really big problem though, was Soonay's grandmother. Her grandmother is probably the biggest part of the reason why she's here. Grandma doesn't like rules. She brings in food and drink, too and has been told about it. But she goes a couple steps further. When we make phone calls, every call that we make is monitored. We have specific people we are allowed to call on our call list and the nurse or the tech dials the number. We even have to keep the phone on speaker so they can monitor. If the call gets too intense, they are allowed to end the call without warning. If the patient speaks a language other than English, they bring in someone who speaks the language.

Soonay and her grandma were trying to get around this rule and I think they were succeeding for a while. Soonay would have the nurse dial her grandma's number, then she would turn up the volume on the TV. When grandma would answer, grandma would do a three way call with someone else who wasn't on the list. That worked until Soonay had a nurse who was paying attention. Soonay went to turn up the volume on the TV and the nurse muted it.

Soonay told her grandma she'd call her back later because this one dayshift nurse actually listened during the calls. Grandma went nuts! She was yelling so loud into the phone that the entire wing could hear what she was saying to the nurse. I'm not sure I would have been able to keep calm, but the nurse did. She finally ended up hanging up on Soonay's grandma after trying to explain to her the rules and why they were there.

The next time her grandmother called she chose to speak their native language, Korean. They didn't realize that one of our nurses is Korean and was able to go in to monitor the call. That really made her grandmother mad. I think Soonay should lose phone call privileges, but that could also be because I don't have anyone I can call.

—

I just found out that girl who had the stuffed animal smuggled in to her died. Her name was Liz. She was fourteen. She wanted to kill herself so badly that a staff member had to sit with her at lunch to make sure she didn't grab any forks or knives. There was one time when she used one of the forks to try to slit her wrists. I actually thought there was supposed to be a staff member with her at all times because she had tried so many times right here in the hospital. It's really sad.

As soon as I heard, I tried to go to Vivian's office to see if I could talk to her. I got halfway there and saw the driver who seems to hate me walking toward me. She was giving me a dirty look, so I decided that I would try to clear the air. That's what being here is all about, right? Learning to make better choices and finding a good way to deal with social stressors?

I stopped walking and said, "Hi. I think we got off on the wrong foot. My name is Storm. What is your name?"

She made a rude snort/grunt noise and said, "I already told you, I know who you are, Pink-Envy."

"Okay, how do you know my real name? No one else here does. And, why are you so angry with me? What have I ever done to you?"

She stood up a little straighter and looked down at me. To be fair, she's a good six inches taller than me without standing up straight. When she straightened up, she looked to be eight inches taller. "My name is Aurora. You have never done anything to me, but from what she has told me, you have bullied my sister and her best friend. I have a problem with that."

Try as I might, I could not think of one single person, aside from Jillian, who I had bullied. And with Jillian, it was less bully and more avenger. "I'm sorry. I have no idea what you're talking about."

"You were in a group home with her not too long ago. You always made fun of her name?"

It felt like alarms and strobe lights went off in my head. I could feel the world shift beneath my feet. "You're Fantasia's sister?"

"Yeah, you little shit. I'm Fantasia's sister. She used to tell me all about you." She kept getting closer and closer to me until she had me backed into the wall. I tried like hell to keep my face blank. With her size and rage, Aurora could crush me no matter how dirty I fight. "So, all I've got to say to you is stay out of my way, don't talk to me, and I will leave you alone."

Given the situation, it felt like good advice. I didn't correct Aurora on the bullying situation. I mean, I was the one Fantasia and Female had been bullying, but it seemed like the wrong thing to say. I also decided against going to talk to Vivian and walked back to my room on legs that felt like rubber.

October 15

I skipped group therapy this morning. I went to breakfast then back to my room to wait for the church service. The first reading was from Isaiah 25:6-10.

I wasn't really paying too much attention until the pastor said, "Death prevailed and swallowed them."

It reminded me that yesterday, Liz died, so I guess death did prevail and swallowed her. He must have realized the unintended impact of that statement on so many of us. Death had taken a stroll through the hallways right next to all of us yesterday and even though none of us had been close to Liz, we were all feeling the loss.

He stopped talking and shuffled through the notes on the lectern. He looked out at all of us and appeared to be struggling to find something to say. He finally asked, "How many of you knew Liz well?"

I looked around the room. There wasn't one single arm raised.

He said, "I see. How many of you know what Taylor Swift wore during her last tour?"

More than half of the people in the room raised their hands.

"This week, I want each of you to reach out and speak to at least one new person every day. Ask them how their day is going, ask them how they are feeling, or if there is anything they need help with. Be kind to one another. If you are struggling with something, ask for help. If you notice someone struggling, offer help. You never know how far one act of kindness might go toward saving a life. Let us pray."

—

I left the church service feeling pretty low. I didn't want to go back to my room to be alone, so I headed down to the stables. Bear had already put all of the horses out to pasture, so I grabbed an apple and a couple sugar cubes and headed over to them. Winona was playing - that's the only way I can describe it. She was running back and forth with another horse. He was all black except for a small white spot right over one of his eyes. They would run together, then one of them would nip at the heels of the other, then they would change direction.

I snacked on the apple as I walked over to stand with Bear. We watched the horses chase each other and play.

He looked at me and smiled. "Do you want another riding lesson?"

"I would love to ride her again!"

Bear whistled and both horses came charging toward him.

All of the animals really love him. He just has this way with them, almost as if he speaks their language. They all seem to trust that he is safe and won't hurt them. I gave each of the horses a sugar cube and we walked them back to the stables where he grabbed the blankets and saddles. We worked together getting the horses ready to ride.

I asked him, "Are you riding with me today?"

He said, "Yes, Lightning needs some exercise, too."

"Is Lightning the most popular name for a horse? I swear there is always at least one horse no matter where you go with the name Lightning."

"I don't know, I think Thunder is used more often than Lightning. Most people who use Lightning use it because of the horse's speed. When I named him, it was because of the white patch over his eye. I thought it looked like a Lightning bolt. It was either name him Lightning or Harry Potter."

"Lightning was a good choice. Don't get me wrong, I love the Harry Potter books and movies. He's magical, but he's too wild for the name. Lightning suits him better."

We mounted up and moved slowly at first. Bear was checking to see what I remembered from earlier in the week. As we rode together, we let our horses pick up speed. I love the feeling of freedom that horseback riding gives me. On Winona's back, I can close my eyes and pretend that I am a cowgirl in the wild west riding herd on my family's cattle. I can feel the sun and wind in my face. I am connected to my horse and we are riding and running together like we are one creature. All too quickly, the freedom ride ends and it's time to bring the horses back to the stable.

Bear and I worked side by side removing all the gear. I'm sure there's a more horsey name for it. I want to learn all about horseback riding and horse care. I have really come to love Winona and wish I could take her with me when I leave here someday. While Bear brought in clean water and feed for the horses, I brushed them down. When I finished with Winona, I leaned into her neck and gave her a hug. She bumped me with her head and nibbled on my shirt. It felt like she was hugging me back. I have fallen head over heels in love with that horse!

October 16

It's Monday again. I feel bad that I didn't do what the pastor asked of us yesterday. Today I am going to step out of my comfort zone and talk to two people I haven't spoken to before. I'll say, "Hi," and ask how they are, or if there is anything I can do for them. That sounds so easy, but how???

I don't trust most people, I don't like many people, and to be completely honest, with the exception of Mr. and Mrs. M, Chloe, Zoe, Eric, Cadence, and Brian, I don't care about how most other people feel. They are the ones that matter to me. I guess I should probably change the way I think, but that's what's helped me stay safe and alive this far.

—

Group therapy this morning was absolutely mind-blowing! Since the first day I met her, I have always thought that Soonay was a little off. She simply doesn't react to things normally. When Liz overdosed the other day, Soonay didn't seem the least bit bothered by it, just kind of, *Oh well*. She didn't start singing *Another One Bites the Dust* but I don't know that I would have been all that surprised.

This morning Soonay shared her story. She just turned fifteen within the last few weeks. She is the second of six children. It seems like a lot of the kids in here come from larger families. I probably would have had a bunch of siblings if mom had lived. Finding placements for more than one of me would have been a nightmare, I'd imagine. I'm difficult enough to place on my own. Soonay's story is one of the worst things I have ever heard. It falls under the heading of a real life horror story. What makes it so much worse is that it's actually true!

Before we got started with our group today, Vivian had us come in and have a moment of silence for Liz. "Does anyone have any stories about Liz that they would like to share? Does anyone have any thoughts or feeling they want to share about what happened with Liz?"

When no one said anything, she said, "Okay, who wants to start working on how to deal with triggers?"

Soonay raised her hand and said, "I'm not sure that I even know what triggers me."

Vivian asked her, "Would you be willing to talk about what brought you here?"

Soonay looked confused and said, "I honestly don't know why I'm here. I was told it was because there was nowhere else to place me."

"Okay, so tell us a little about your family before you came here," Vivian said.

Soonay is tiny. When I say tiny, I don't think she's even five feet tall and she might weigh ninety pounds. She's also really pretty. She has this porcelain doll look to her. She reminds me of one of those little Asian dolls in the glass cases that you see in Chinese restaurants. I'm pretty sure she said she is Korean.

She was sitting in her chair with one leg dangling, the other one up on the seat. When after a few minutes, Soonay still hadn't started talking, Vivian prompted her, "Are you sure you want to talk about it?"

"Oh, yes," she said. "I was trying to figure out how to get started." She scrunched her nose up and said, "Mother was very passionate about raising good children. She always made sure she disciplined us when we did something wrong. We were born to be obedient children and she would not have us any other way. Grandma disciplined her and her siblings when they were little. Someday, if I have them, I will discipline my children. Discipline can be short or it can last for a long time. For my older sister, it lasted a long time."

I wasn't entirely sure where she was going with this, but I could already feel the hair on the back of my neck and on my arms rising. I was hoping she wasn't going to say what I was almost positive she was going to say.

"My sister was very beautiful. She had a lot of boyfriends. When she was fourteen, Mother found out that she had been having sex. There was a positive pregnancy test in the bathroom trash can. She always told us that we were a team. When one of us had a problem, we all shared the problem. That way no one suffered alone.

"When Mother found the test, she lined us up from youngest to oldest against the living room wall. She has a bamboo riding whip that she uses when we are bad. She can use it to hit two of us or more at a time. She started at my older sister and just kept hitting us down the line. I don't remember how long she kept going. At one point, my youngest sister, Nia, couldn't stand up anymore. Her legs just gave out and down she went. Mother stopped next to her and screamed at her to get up.

"Nia just laid there. She didn't make any noise, just laid there. Mother kept hitting her with the whip. She even kicked her a few times to get her to answer her. My older sister, Mina, stepped in front of Mother and got hit in the face with the whip.

"I'm not sure if Mother even knew she was still swinging the whip. Mina's face had been sliced open and there was blood everywhere. Grandma came into the room and saw what was happening. She grabbed Mother's wrist and got her to stop swinging at us. She took Mina to the hospital for stitches, and told Mother to start cleaning up her mess."

Soonay stopped talking for a minute and looked off into space. The rest of us sat there staring at her in disbelief. I'm pretty sure that my mouth was hanging open. When Soonay started speaking again, the room was so quiet, I could make out the sounds of the nurses moving around in the hallways outside.

"Mother had me try to wake Nia. Her back was bleeding

from where the whip had hit her, but she wasn't moving, not even when I pressed against the cuts on her back. I saw Mother feel her neck and bend down to listen to her. She asked me to run upstairs and get one of the sheets from Nia's bed. The sheet I pulled was yellow and white checked. I brought it downstairs and saw Mother sitting on the sofa rocking Nia. She looked so tiny. She was just laying there with her arms out to the side and her head back. She could have been a bigger version of one of my baby dolls.

"Mother had me spread the sheet on the floor and we wrapped Nia in it. We wrapped her whole body. Mama made me leave Nia and go out to the shed with her. She picked out two shovels and took me to the far side of the backyard away from the windows of the neighbors, and told me to start digging. We dug for a long time before Mother said it was deep enough. Then she went inside and got Nia. We covered her up with dirt and later Mother planted a rosebush there."

Vivian asked her, "Your mother made you help her bury your sister after she killed her?"

Soonay shrugged and said, "Mother needed help and we had been bad. It was a lot harder when we had to bury Mina."

"I'm sorry, what?" Vivian had a look of absolute horror on her face.

"I was twelve when we buried Nia. We buried Mina last year."

Vivian interrupted her. "What happened to the baby?"

"Nia? She died."

"No, Mina's baby. You said there was a positive pregnancy test."

"Oh, I don't know. I think she lost the baby early on. She ended up with twenty-six stitches in her cheek."

"How old was Nia?"

"She was four." Everything Soonay said was in a calm, conversational tone. Almost like this was a normal thing. She was talking about her mother torturing and killing her kids and then making the siblings help her bury them. I know how bad my mom messed me up, but Soonay is probably the most damaged human being I have ever met. I don't think she can be fixed and what I find to be truly terrifying about her is that all of this seems normal! She has no concept that this is not how a family is supposed to work – not that I am the family expert, but even I know when there is a messed up family dynamic.

She went on to tell us how a year after her mom killed her little sister, Nia, she ended Mina's life also. In another attempt to "discipline" her children, Soonay's mom went too far and Mina died. From the story she was telling, Soonay's mom and grandma frequently withheld food, which could be part of the reason why she is so tiny. I think Mina was probably really weak from malnutrition and whatever horrific beating her mother gave her was too much for her to handle.

The really sick thing is her mother made Soonay help her bury both bodies! She killed her kids in front of the others and made them help her clean up her mess. It was easier for her to cover up the death of the four-year-old. She had been born at

home and it sounds like there was no legal record of her exis-
tence. Mina was different. She had been fifteen, in high school
and had an after school job.

When Mina stopped going to school, her teachers noticed.
She had been quiet in school, but got good grades and was
never a behavior problem. The school sent social workers out
to her house and questioned the kids when the mom wasn't
home. One of the younger siblings led the social worker into
the backyard by her hand and pointed to the graves of the two
sisters. One had a rosebush growing from it, the other had a
camelia planted. Soonay said the police arrived with cadaver
dogs and within the course of a few hours, the bodies had been
dug up, her mom was arrested, and she was removed from the
home. The siblings were sent to different placements so they
could all receive intensive therapy. The "authorities" thought
they might be better off not placed together, especially as they
were certain that if there was even a slight chance for adoption,
it wouldn't be with them together as a sibling group.

Vivian ended our therapy session after Soonay's story. I'm
pretty sure she went home for the day.

October 17

This morning I got pulled into the social worker's office. She said she wanted to talk to me about a possible placement. I told her that if I got sent anywhere other than back to Mr. and Mrs. M I would run. She tried to talk to me in her best "I'm an adult, I know what's best for you" voice. I wish these people knew just how stupid they sound.

I mean, seriously? How can they possibly know what's best for me? I know I've said it before, but I think it bears repeating. How can you know what's best for me if you don't even know me? It doesn't matter. She just kept right on talking at me. I shut down and ignored her.

She finally put her hand on my shoulder and gave me a little shake. When I looked up at her she asked me if I had heard anything she had just said. I told her, "No," I wasn't listening to her. I'm sure that pissed her off, but who cares? If they aren't going to listen to me, there's no way I'm going to listen to them. I'm pretty sure she was telling me about the wonderful family that she was placing me with next.

When she dismissed me from her office, she told me to make sure that I had the items in my room packed and ready to go, because I could be leaving at any minute. Twenty minutes later one of the nurses came to my room and asked me if I was ready. I really wasn't. Okay, if I were being told I was returning to Sylva and the McClellands, they wouldn't have been able to hold me back. To be honest, I probably would have run over anyone standing in the hallway.

I know that when I got to Sylva, I had myself convinced that it wasn't going to be any different than any other placement I'd been in. I told myself that I wouldn't let them get into my heart, that I wouldn't care about them. So far, they are the only family I have ever cared about. I would say I would try to run away and find my way back to them, but it's more than a five hour car ride from here, it would probably take me two weeks to walk there.

I grabbed my backpack of belongings and followed the nurse to the entrance of the hospital. A DSS worker stood there waiting for me. She had a clipboard in her hands, signing what I'm sure were my discharge papers.

All I could think was *Here we go again.* I was pissed that I wasn't going to be allowed to say goodbye to Vivian. She'd been my best therapist so far. I didn't even bother to ask, I knew the answer would be no. I don't even know her last name.

The lady looked at me and said, "Hi Storm, I'm Leesa. I'm going to be taking you to your next placement."

I walked past her toward the exit, muttering "Hey." I really didn't care what her name was or where I was going. I didn't plan on being there long. I heard the click of the magnetic lock releasing and I pushed the door open.

I kept walking even though I didn't know which car I should be looking for. Leesa scrambled out after me and had to run to keep up. She directed me to a boring older model beige Honda. It was kinda perfect for her – matched her clothes and what I'm sure was probably a beige personality, too - blah.

Fifteen minutes after pulling out of the parking lot of the mental hospital, Leesa was pulling up in front of a house that looked like a good solid wind would blow it over. There was a front porch, but part of the railing was missing, and the part that wasn't, was leaning dangerously over the side. There was one lonely tree that looked like it was dying in the dirt yard – the leaves it had shed littered the sandy front yard, but there was no grass. If it's possible, the property looked depressed. When I got out of the car, Leesa directed me to a door on the side of the house. From there, I could look into the backyard and see a clothesline with all four lines snapped in different places, and a chain link fence with a section missing out of it. The steps leading up to the back door were two large cinder blocks.

I'm not sure what I was expecting, but I guess living in the huge house in Sylva spoiled me some. Even while sharing a room with Cadence I still had a lot of space to myself. The house that Leesa brought me to could have fit inside Mr. and

Mrs. M's house three times. I remember being told that in order to foster, there has to be at least one hundred and twenty square feet of space per child in the house. That doesn't mean that each child gets their own space that size, but that if there are ten people living in the house, the house has to be at lease twelve hundred square feet, The lady fostering here was pushing it to the limit. I was child number eight and guess how large the house was: twelve hundred square feet.

Leesa introduced the woman as Misty. Misty was in her mid-thirties with a chin length blonde bob that looked like it had just been blown out at the salon. She was decked out in Michael Kors from the scarf on her neck all the way down to the peep toe pumps that showed off perfectly polished toenails. Her makeup was flawless, making her skin look airbrushed. She didn't look like she belonged in this rundown looking house. She said that she has been fostering kids for a long time and that I should like it here. Leesa and Misty talked for a few minutes then Leesa left. No goodbye, no good luck, she just left.

After the door closed behind Leesa, Misty took me on a two minute tour of the house and showed me the room where I would be sleeping. There were two sets of bunk beds in both of the 'kid' bedrooms. The arrangement didn't leave a whole lot of room to move. There was a tall chest of drawers in my room with four drawers. One drawer per person. I don't have that much, but only one drawer will make things kind of tight. It's really going to limit the amount of clothing I can have – assuming, of course, that I am able to get any new clothes.

I put my backpack on the bottom bunk of the bed I was sharing with one of the other kids. Misty told me that was my assigned sleeping space. The other girls were all in school so I would meet them later. I went in search of Misty. When I found her, she handed me a printout of the house rules – up at the very top was, *No running away.* Yeah, right.

—

This is not going to work for me. I have had to remind Misty of my name several times since I got here. The last time I tried to tell her she held up her hand and told me this is just an emergency placement, I won't be here long enough for it to matter. I really hope that's the case. Since that last exchange, she told me she was busy and to just go sit and watch TV until she found something for me to do.

There isn't much to this house. When you walk in the side door, you walk into the kitchen. She has all of the cabinets labeled. Then there is a cabinet that's labeled *Kids' stuff.* That one has those little seven day pill packets – you know the ones where you have your meds all portioned out for the day, everyday of the week. There are seven of them in the cabinet, each with a different name label on it. If I weren't planning on taking off tonight I'm sure she'd end up making one for me, too. I saw an extra one sitting next to the sink. It looked like there had been a name label on it that had been partially peeled off.

When you walk through the kitchen, you go straight into the den. The den has a sofa that looks like it was salvaged from

Goodwill twenty years ago. The material is threadbare and there is even duct tape holding the stuffing in one of the arms. There were two mismatched wooden end tables that were scuffed. Each table had a lamp that looked like something out of *That 70's Show*, the bases of the lamps were tarnished brass. The shades were a weird gold material with a burnt orange velvet trim around the top and bottom of the shade. There was an oval coffee table in front of the sofa. It had cigarette burn marks across the top of it. The only nice object in the den was the smart TV.

I was sitting on the sofa streaming old episodes of *Grey's Anatomy* when the other kids started coming home. The first girl who walked through the door called back behind her and said, "I told you there would be a new one when we got home."

Apparently, there had been another girl here yesterday. She either went back to her family or to a forever home. There are some days when I feel like it might be easier being a dog. People are always in a hurry to adopt a dog and take them to their forever home. The ones who don't get adopted end up being put to sleep. I am not suicidal in the least, but there are times when I wonder if just like dogs who stay too long in the shelter, would it be better if we kids got put down. It would certainly eliminate the overcrowding of the throwaways like me in the hospital.

By the time all seven of the other girls got back from school, Misty had gone out to get dinner. The girl who said the thing about 'a new one' told me her name was Sue. While Misty was out getting us food, Sue gave me the rundown on the house situation. All the girls in the house have a chore - mow the lawn, do the laundry, cook dinner, clean. Misty goes grocery shopping and every couple of months takes one or two of the girls to Goodwill for new clothes.

I asked Sue what Misty does for a living and she looked at me like I belonged in the mental hospital I just left.

"What do you mean, what does she do? This is it, she fosters kids. She always has eight girls that she collects checks for. If she had a bigger house, she'd have more kids."

That made me furious! Foster parents are given a monthly stipend for caring for foster kids. For kids thirteen and older, the going rate right now in North Carolina is eight hundred ten dollars. And of course, all eight of us are over thirteen. Misty is making over six thousand dollars a month, tax free off of us! I already hate her.

October 18

Misty doesn't have a security system, thankfully. All of my belongings were still in the backpack, which I hid after dinner when no one was around. For a house with nine females living in it, Misty's is the quietest house I have ever been in. None of the girls really talk to each other. Misty doesn't really care if we get to know one another, or interact. As long as we do the chores she has assigned to us, and she can collect her checks, she really doesn't care.

Around two in the morning, the house was quiet. I could hear Misty snoring loudly in her room. She should probably be checked out to make sure she doesn't have sleep apnea. The other three girls in my room were sleeping soundly, if not as loudly. I left the room and closed the door silently behind me, praying that none of the floorboards creaked. I grabbed my backpack from behind the sofa, unlocked the side door, and slipped out of the house.

I had checked the map earlier and knew that there was about

a thirty minute walk from the house to the Wilmington River-walk. I didn't know exactly what I was going to do when I got there, but it was a starting point. It was dark out, but nothing like the darkness when I tried to run away in Sylva. The animal sounds that I could hear out here were the occasional dog barking and the screeching of cats fighting. I walked down the street and thought about how different each of the places were that I had lived, and run away from. Here in Wilmington, the air smelled different than it had in Sylva. This close to the ocean, there was a salty taste to it and it felt heavier. I'm not really sure how else to describe it, other than it felt like a wet heaviness in the air – like a not quite dry blanket had been wrapped around me. I was just happy that it wasn't cold out.

I made it to the Riverwalk pretty quickly. I walked for a while longer looking for a bench that I could curl up on. I figured I'd nap for a bit and then find some food and get moving. I was starting to get tired, so I stopped at a restaurant that had picnic tables with big umbrellas. I figured it was as good a place as any to hide for a bit and sleep.

I curled up on the bench of one of the tables and looked out over the water. There were lights lining the riverwalk, and bugs flying close to the lights. I watched as bats seemed to dance around the lights, occasionally swooping down to feast on the bugs for dinner. I closed my eyes and listened to the sounds of the Cape Fear River as I drifted off to sleep.

I woke up just as the sun was starting to creep over the horizon. I left the shelter of the picnic table and started walking around looking for a gas station or convenience store. I was really hungry and was hoping I'd be able to grab something. I saw a Scotchman convenience store at a gas station and went in. I used the bathroom and washed my hands and face. I brushed and braided my hair and tried to make myself look like I hadn't just spent the night sleeping on a picnic table bench. The shop owners don't pay as much attention to you if you look well groomed.

I walked through the aisles picking up different things that I would be able to eat without heating; a can of tuna, chef Bo-yardee ravioli, a candy bar. I almost made it. I'm pretty sure the guy behind the counter never noticed me swiping the food. The problem is I never noticed the police officer come in. I made sure my clothes didn't have any weird bulky spots and I was about to leave when I heard a voice behind me ask, "Are you planning on paying for any of those things?"

I thought about running, but when my body tensed to take off, he grabbed me. I could have tried to get away from him, but he was built like a tank and had a grip like a vise. It was over. I had just been caught shoplifting. I used to be so much better at this. I have really lost my touch! He made me empty my pockets and pull out the items I'd stashed in my backpack. He asked me for ID. When I told him I didn't have any he asked me for my name and date of birth. I told him my name was Storm Rogers and that I was eighteen. He handcuffed me, put me in the backseat and took my backpack.

The ride to the police department was uncomfortably quiet. He didn't seem like much of a conversationalist, and I wasn't talking – I've seen way too many episodes of *Law and Order to* know that it's better to keep my mouth shut. He had asked me before we got into the car where I belonged. I told him nowhere. I sat in the backseat listening to the chatter on the police radio. The officer was listening to two different channels at the same time. I asked him at one point how he could understand what was happening.

He just shrugged and said, "You get used to it."

Once we got to the station, he put me in a small room and asked me if I wanted anything to eat or drink. I shrugged, trying to act tough, and then my stomach betrayed me by growling. He told me to wait and closed the door. I was going to try to sneak out, but there was no doorknob. I paced around the room for a few minutes then finally slumped down in one of the chairs. I put my backpack on the table and put my head down on it. I was asleep in seconds.

The next time the door opened the officer came in with some hot chocolate and a warm cinnamon bun. He said, "One of the wives brings us fresh pastries almost every day. I thought you might be hungry, so I brought you something to eat."

"Thank you."

He sat down across from me and pulled a little notepad out of his pocket and clicked his pen. "I am Officer Burns. I want to help you, but I need you to give me some information. What is your name?"

I picked at the cinnamon bun and kept thinking how stupid I was for getting caught. I guess there is the argument that maybe I shouldn't have been stealing in the first place, but I was hungry and really had no idea how long it would be before I would get another meal. Officer Burns didn't say anything. He just sat there. Watching me.

I finally sighed and said, "Okay, my name is Storm Rogers."

"Good," he said. "We have a starting point. Storm, where do you live?"

"I already told you, nowhere."

He scrubbed his face with his hands and said, "Okay, hear me out. I just picked you up for shoplifting. I know you aren't eighteen. My guess is you ran away from home last night. You're too clean to have been out on the street any longer than that. Talk to me, tell me what happened."

He seemed really nice. I had always heard horror stories from other kids about how the cops treated them. I've never really had any problems with them. My experience with them has always been that as long as you weren't being a jerk, they were pretty cool, too. Most of the time, anyway. Thinking back on it, the kids who complained that the officers were jerks were the problem kids anyway. The last one who told me how bad they were was Shiquita - and that was after she beat the crap out of Fina and her friends.

"I'm a foster kid."

He sat across from me and waited for me to say more. When

I didn't he said, "Okay. So that's part of the story."

"I was pretty sure that explained everything."

He took in a breath, closed his eyes and blew it out. "Storm, the part where I asked you to tell me what happened, well, that was where there needed to be a story. You saying you're a foster kid? That is not a story. I don't want you to bullshit me. I want to help you and I am trying to be patient here, because I feel like you have to potential to be a good kid, but my patience has limits and we are very quickly approaching those limits. So I am going to ask you one last time, what happened?"

I studied Officer Burns' face and could tell he really did want to help me. I said, "Okay. Yesterday I was discharged from Oceanside, you know, the mental hospital? I was there after having beaten up a girl at school who slapped my foster sister. I got discharged and sent to live with this fake, bleached blonde who has eight foster kids so she doesn't have to work. I didn't want to be in that kind of environment so I took off."

Officer Burns sat for a second then said, "You know I have to take you back."

"Can't you just let me go and pretend you didn't find me?"

He just gave me a look.

Another officer knocked on the door then opened it. "Hey, what's the name of the kid you've got here?"

"Storm, why?"

"We've got a missing juvenile report." He looked at his notepad. "A Pink-Envy Serenity Rogers, white female, fourteen. Ran away from a foster care placement overnight."

Both officers looked over at me. Officer Burns said, "I thought you said your name was Storm."

"I'm sorry. I don't go by my first name. I have been using the name Storm for years, so that's how I introduce myself. I mean, if your first name were Pink-Envy, would you tell people?"

Officer Burns laughed and said, "Probably not. Okay, fair enough."

"I want to have it legally changed when I turn eighteen."

Officer Burns told the other officer to call Misty and tell her that I had been found. He would be returning me to her house after he finished talking to me. It was so unfair. I know that Misty couldn't care less about whether I'm there as long as she's receiving a check for me. I'll bet that if I hadn't just gotten there yesterday, she wouldn't have filed a report. I knew I'd have to go back, but having had that freedom for just a few hours was really nice.

Officer Burns said, "Come on. I'll take you back."

"Do I have to go?" I hated the whiny sound to my voice, but I felt like I was about to cry and I didn't like it.

"Yeah, kiddo, you've got to go. Come on, it can't be that bad. She cares enough to file a missing persons report on you."

"She just didn't want to miss out on my portion of her check. Although, I'm sure that as soon as I'm out the door, there will be another girl to take my place."

Officer Burns frowned but didn't say anything. The ride back to the house was pretty quiet. When we got there, before he walked me up to the door, he gave me his card with a cellphone number on it. He said, "If you are ever in trouble and you need anything, you call me. I think you're a good kid and I want to see you succeed."

"Thank you."

He walked me up to the door and rang the bell. Misty answered the door and really turned on the drama. "Oh my gosh, Serena! I've been so worried about you!"

"My name is Storm."

She ignored me and started talking to Officer Burns. "Oh, thank you so much for finding her. I have been worried sick. I didn't expect her to run off after only one day with me." She got very close to him and put one hand on his arm while the other played with a button on her blouse. She said kind of breathlessly, "I can't thank you enough. Is there anything I can offer you? Anything I can get you? Maybe some coffee or breakfast?"

Officer Burns took a step back, away from her, cleared his throat and said, "No, thank you, Ma'am. I'm good. Storm, take care of yourself."

"Yes, sir."

Misty stood with her hand on my shoulder on the porch while we watched Officer Burns drive off. Once he was gone, her fingernails dug into my shoulder. Through clenched teeth she said, "You ungrateful little bitch. Get in the house right now!"

I stepped onto the top step heading toward the door and she pushed me hard. I tripped over the entry and fell. My face hit the hardwood floor and exploded with pain. As I was trying to get up, I heard her come into the house and slam the door.

"I cannot believe that you ran away after less than twenty-four hours in my house. Were you selling your body out on the street corner? Maybe buying drugs and getting high with a John? Let me tell you how things work in my house. You follow the rules. That's it." She punctuated her last remark with a swift kick to my ribs.

I curled into a fetal position, trying desperately to catch my breath. Once the waves of pain stopped crashing over me, I sat up, but stayed on the floor. I gingerly touched the side of my face where my cheek had connected. The bones under my skin felt crunchy. Misty nudged me with her foot. "Get up," she shouted.

I stood slowly banding my arm around my ribs and said, "I feel dizzy. My face and my side hurt."

"Shut up. Just go to your room while I figure out what I'm going to do about you."

I slowly bent down to pick up my backpack then shuffled back to the room. I closed the door and crawled into my space on the bottom bunk. I curled into as tight a ball as my injuries would allow while holding on for dear life to my backpack. I sobbed as quietly as I could until I fell asleep.

October 19

I woke up this morning to Misty yelling at one of the other girls. I heard Sue mutter something about how glad she was that it wasn't her. Then she swung her legs over the side of the bed. She told me that I should probably start getting ready for school. I stayed in bed. I didn't see the point in getting up.

Misty crashed through the door to our room bellowing for everyone to get up. She's such a tiny person, it's hard to believe that she is able to make that much noise. When I started to get up, she took one look at my face and said, "You are staying home today. There is no way you are going out into public looking like that."

Sue glanced at my face, did a double take and gasped. Once I was able to get in front of a mirror, I saw what all the fuss was about. The left side of my face looked like I had gone a few rounds with a kickboxer. It was puffy and swollen and my cheek right under my eye was an eggplant shade of purple.

I said to Misty, "I bet you don't want people seeing this.

They'd ask me what happened and I'd feel obligated to tell the truth. Wouldn't that cut into your payday?"

Misty's face turned red. "Why you little shit! I didn't do that to you!"

"I wouldn't have fallen if you hadn't pushed me through the doorway. So, yeah, it's your fault. You did it."

Misty launched herself across the room and smacked my face hard enough that I stumbled backwards and fell on my butt.

I looked up at her from the floor and said, "Thank you. Now both sides of my face will match."

Misty said, "I cannot with you. You will stay here in this room today." There was venom dripping from her words. "I am serious. If you step one toe through this doorway and I catch you, I will chain you to the bed myself!"

She stormed out of the room and I crawled back into bed. I listened to the sounds of the rest of the house getting ready for their day. I didn't care. I just wanted to go to sleep and not wake up. My face was really sore, my nose was running, and I had a headache. I wiped my hand across my nose to stop it from running. When I pulled my hand away it was covered in blood. Great! Misty will probably freak out because I got blood on her pillowcase.

I went to the bathroom to clean myself up. I didn't hear anyone moving around in the house anymore and was hoping Misty had gone. The face looking back at me from the mirror was Halloween scary. The right side of my face was bruised and swollen, the left side of my face had an angry red handprint, and I had dried, crusted blood around my nostrils. I definitely looked like I had been on the losing end of a kickboxing match. I couldn't even joke about *you should see the other guy.*

Once I had cleaned myself up and made sure there was no blood left on the bathroom sink, I looked outside. Misty's car was gone. I went to the front door, but the deadbolt had been thrown, and I didn't have a key. The backdoor's deadbolt had been locked, too. I went in search of a phone. Misty didn't have a landline. I was hoping that maybe one of the girls had a cellphone that had been left behind. Not likely, I know, but I had to try. When I didn't find a phone I started looking at the windows and the screens. In the other bedroom, there was a window without a screen. Even luckier, this window hadn't been nailed shut like some of the others. I could open the window and escape! As quickly as my injuries would let me, I went back to my room, grabbed my backpack and went through the window.

I started walking with no plan. When I was a block away from the house, I saw an Urgent Care. I went in thinking that this was probably the safest place for me to hide.

The nurse behind the desk took one look at my face and immediately pulled me back to a room. "Honey, who did this to you?"

"Her name is Misty," I said. "She runs my foster home."

"Your foster mom did this to your face?"

"I'm not going to call her a foster mom," I said. "She's more like a demon who takes in teenage girls for a paycheck."

"I want the doctor to take a look at your face and maybe get an X-ray. I want to rule out any facial fractures. Will you stay here? I promise you are not in any trouble."

I agreed to wait and hopped up on the exam table. I must have fallen asleep because I never even heard the doctor come in.

And right behind him was Officer Burns. "Storm? What happened?"

The doctor said, "Do you know this young lady?"

Officer Burns said, "Yes, we met just yesterday. She's a good kid."

The doctor did his exam, took X-rays, and said I had several fractures around my eyes. He wanted me to go to the emergency room for a CAT scan. Officer Burns said he would drive me. On our way out, I thanked the nice nurse who had taken care of me. I never got her name or the doctor's.

———

"What happened?" I could tell Officer Burns was really mad. His jaw was clenched and there was a muscle in his cheek that was jumping.

"When you dropped me off yesterday, Misty grabbed me and shoved me into the house. I tripped and fell on my face. This morning she slapped me so hard my nose started bleeding. I think she left to take the other girls to school. When I found a window without a screen, I went through the window and walked to the Urgent Care."

"You know that I have to make a report about all of this?"

"I know. I want you to. I don't want to have to go back there."

"I can't make you any promises about where you will go, Storm," he said quietly. "What I can promise is that I believe you and I will do everything I can to make sure Misty is charged with assault." He was sitting on a chair with me in the emergency room. Of course, because he brought me in, they took us straight back to the psych unit – they just assumed that it was a behavioral health issue.

He pulled out the little notepad he kept in his uniform pocket and called over the radio for a report number. When the dispatcher asked him what type of report it was going to be, he said assault. I could feel the tears streaming down my cheeks. He actually believed me!

He wrote down the report number, walked over to the door to my room and asked if someone could bring us some tissues. He handed me the tissues and said, "Let's go from the beginning. Tell me everything that happened - Don't make anything up or try to make it sound bigger or better, just tell me what happened."

—

One of the ER docs came in, gently examined my face and got a head scan. He told me that the way the bones had fractured, I had been very lucky - there was no brain bleed and I wouldn't need surgery, the bones should heal on their own. If there is any such thing as a lucky broken facial bone, I guess this would be it.

Officer Burns had taken several pictures of my face and wrote his report. I heard him talking to one of the nurses saying that he needed to go to the magistrate's office for warrants. I didn't want him to leave me. They were speaking softly enough that I couldn't hear everything, but I caught a few snippets and it sounded like I was not going to have to go back to Misty. Now, if she got arrested for assault, that would mean DSS would have to find places for Sue and the other girls.

The doctor had given me some medicine for pain and I had asked for something that would make me sleep. I really want to escape this nightmare.

I slept.

October 20

It's hard to keep track of the time in here. There are no windows and no clocks on the walls. It could be three in the morning or five in the afternoon. I'm in the room right next to the nurses' station, it seems like I'm always in the room right next to the nurses' station, and the lights are always on outside of my room. The only way I can tell what time of the day it is, is by the group of nurses that are working.

When I woke up I could tell that it was daytime. The dayshift nurses are really loud and sound like they have fun working together. I'm pretty sure it was their laughter that woke me up. One of them was talking about her vacation with her family – they went on a Disney cruise to the Caribbean. I listened to her talk about how much fun she had with her daughters during their lunches with their favorite characters. They even went to some island where they swam with pigs! Imagine that – ocean swimming pigs!

All I could think of was how amazing it would be to be able

to go sit with my mom and my sisters while having lunch with Merida from Brave or maybe even Goofy. I'm not sure who Cadence would have wanted, but I feel like the twins would have wanted Snow White, Cinderella, or Aurora. I imagined having my mom braid our hair and fuss over our clothes. When I looked out of my room at the nurse who was talking, I could imagine that she would have done that very thing. She would have worked out every detail right down to the perfect bubbly drinks for toasts and napkins that matched the place settings.

I closed my eyes and continued to listen to her vacation adventures. She talked about how they had started their vacation by visiting the Kennedy Space Center at Port Canaveral in Florida. She said she hadn't wanted to go there but her husband had always dreamed of seeing the Space Shuttle Atlantis and experiencing the shuttle launch. She talked about how much the kids loved it. She even said that as little as she had wanted to do it, she loved that it made her husband so happy. I could see Mrs. M doing something just like that, going and doing something she didn't think she would enjoy knowing that the activity would bring Mr. M joy. She would end up having fun anyway because of how happy it made him.

Their conversation was interrupted by a really loud crash and then screaming. I heard a voice yell for security right about the same time that an overhead page went out for a security alert. I moved as close as I could to the door to try and see what was happening. My sitter wasn't paying any attention to me, since she was watching the action, too. Another kid down the hall from me was freaking out. He was screaming and started ripping things off of the walls. I saw the trashcan fly out of the room. He actually picked it up and threw it over the nurses' station desk. He punched at the paper towel dispenser and started breaking off pieces of plastic. He got one of the pieces into his hand, stabbed his arm and started digging the shard of plastic down through his skin. Bright red blood started going everywhere. One of the security guards got him from behind and somehow managed to fall backwards into the recliner in the boy's room. The guard was huge – easily over six feet tall, while the boy wasn't much more than five feet tall.

The guard had wrapped one of his arms around the kid so that the hand with the plastic shard was immobilized against the boy's body. The guard had the kid's legs sandwiched in between his. I watched as the guard squeezed the boy's hand and shook his arm until the shard dropped.

While that was happening, one of the nurses had grabbed the kid's bleeding arm and had clamped her hand over the cut that was spurting blood everywhere. Another nurse had grabbed a shot of some kind of medicine and jabbed it into the kid's hip.

I heard the guard say, "Please don't miss – I don't want to get shot with that."

Within just a few minutes, the kid was asleep.

The guard placed the kid on the bed while the one nurse continued to hold onto his wrist. There were security guards everywhere and a tiny woman I found out later was the doctor, came running in asking what happened. The kid was rushed out of the area on his stretcher. I guess he was going to have to have surgery. When everyone cleared out, I saw blood all over the room. It was everywhere: it had splatter across the floor, spurted up the wall. It had even hit the ceiling.

Some methed out asshole walked past the kid's room laughed and said, "Hahaha, that little fucker stuck himself good." I wanted to punch him in the throat. My sitter told me that she needed me to get back from the door. I really didn't want to see anything else anyway, so I got back in bed and asked her to turn on my TV. It turned on to *Law and Order: Special Victims Unit.*

———

I woke up later on to one of the nurse aides taking my vital signs. She apologized for waking me up and asked if I needed anything. I said, "No," and when she was done, I rolled over and curled up in a ball. I listened to the sounds of the unit and cried. I could hear the methed out guy from earlier start fighting with one of the nurses, which made security come running again. Someone hit their panic button so an overhead page went out again. I heard one of the nurses yelling for restraints while another one said something about drawing up meds. I feel like I'm always on this same roller coaster ride. I know that a lot of this is my own doing – I mean, I'd be in a house in sort of my own bed right now if I hadn't run away from Misty's house. But staying with Misty wasn't the answer, either.

I wonder over and over if this is going to be my life until I'm eighteen. Am I destined to go to the hospital, be discharged to a crappy foster or group home and then screw up so that I get sent back to the hospital? This time it wasn't even my screw up, but there is no place that will take me. I wonder if the other girls are still with Misty. I don't want to live like this, but I have no idea how to break this cycle. Maybe it would have been better if I had never met the McClellands. Then I wouldn't know what I was missing. I wouldn't have had a taste of what it meant to be a part of a real family.

October 21

This morning one of the nurses came in and asked if I wanted to take a shower today. As soon as she mentioned a shower, I realized that my last shower was before I left the hospital almost a week ago. I didn't even want to smell myself.

Here's the thing about living in the emergency room. Because I came in as a "behavioral problem" (even though this time I really wasn't) I have to be escorted everywhere by security and one of the nursing staff, whether it's a nurse aide or a nurse. Most of the time it's a nurse aide, but today I got one of the nurses. She's the one in charge today. She talked to me and treated me like a human, not just some waste of space who should apologize for taking up her time.

She said to me, "My name is Maria. I'm the assistant nurse manager here. I'm going to be helping my nurses take care of you while you are here. Do you understand why you are here?"

I said, "Yes. I ran away from Misty's house and told the truth, that she assaulted me. I'd rather go live on the street than ever have to go back there."

Maria stopped walking and said, "Oh, you aren't going back there. I do believe the officer who brought you in was able to arrest her. He took your statement, pictures of your injuries. Honey, she's never going to be able to foster again. That gravy train dried up for her."

"Good!"

"The hospital social workers and DSS are still looking for a placement for you. While that is happening, you have some work to do."

I looked at her and made a face. "What do you mean?"

Maria said, "I've read through your chart. You have a long history of getting into a placement, getting into a fight or running away and then being sent to the hospital as a behavior problem. Once you get to the hospital you lose your placement and then the cycle starts over. Not including hospitals, you've been in three different placements in the last three months! Something has to give, or you will to continue going 'round and 'round on this carousel ride until you age out of the system."

It was as if she had been reading my mind - or my diary. That is the one thing I have been able to hold onto no matter where I've been. "I want very much to get off of this ride. I was thinking about that last night when that meth head started flipping out."

Maria let me into the bathroom where I was able to shower. The hot water felt so good! I feel like there are a lot of things that kids who live with their real parents just take for granted.

A nice hot shower is one of them. In the group homes, if you don't get to the shower early enough, you don't get any hot water. Sometimes, there's another kid who wants the shower while you're in it and they jump you so they can take your turn. In one of my group homes, another girl almost stabbed me because I got to the shower before she did.

I would love to be able to choose my own body wash and shampoo. I know it sounds silly, but I've never done that. Nobody has ever said, "Hey let's go to Bath and Body Works and pick out something that smells pretty for you." I have to admit, though, I think Maria and the other nurses may have gone out of their way to get me a lavender Johnson and Johnson body wash. It smells really nice.

After getting dressed in the clean scrubs, I walked back to the unit with Maria and the security guard. I told Maria, "I don't know how to break the cycle. I mean, I know I have to change and quit running away, but I don't know how to change."

Maria said, "We can help you build some coping skills while you're here, maybe go over some of the patterns you've had in the past and figure out what you can do differently."

I told her, "I was happy with the McClellands. They said they wanted to adopt me. That was even after I beat up the other girl at school. I know what I did was wrong. I just really want to go home." By the time I was done, I was crying. Thankfully we had gotten back to my room, so I could crawl into bed and finish my ugly, snotty crying with only the sitter to watch me. She was sweet, though. She had someone grab some tissues and water and brought them in to me. She smoothed my hair out of my face and asked if I would like a cool washcloth. When I didn't answer her, I heard her direct someone out in the hallway to grab her a washcloth. She ran it under some cold water, wrung it out and gently wiped off my face. She told me that when I was feeling up to it, she would love to braid my hair, if I would like.

I heard one of the nurses say, "Hey Erica, you never got to finish telling us about your vacation. What all did you do?"

I listened to Erica, the nurse, talk about how her family went on a glass bottomed boat in the Caribbean at a place called Castaway Cay. They snorkeled with stingrays and took pictures and videos underwater. She squealed when she talked about how excited her five-year-old daughter was that one of the stingrays ate right out of her hand.

She said at their next port stop they swam with the dolphins. How magical would that be? I'd feel just like Ariel, only I'd never want to grow legs. I would swim with the dolphins and play underwater forever!

October 22

Last night I heard the nurses talking about that kid who slit his wrist. He was another one who came here for behavioral problems. They called him Jason, and it sounds like a lot of them really liked him. Jason had been living in a group home and got really mad at his roommate. I think almost all of us who have lived in group homes have some type of anger management trouble.

Anyway, Jason's roommate said a bunch of really awful things to him. He said that he was going to break out of the home and go find Jason's mom and his little sister and stab them to death.

Jason didn't respond well to that. He somehow got a hold of a butcher knife from the kitchen and went after the roommate with it. The group home staff tried to de-escalate things. One of the staff members was injured and Jason ended up here for evaluation. Funny thing is, he has a real mom.

When he was originally brought in, Jason didn't qualify

for the kids' psych unit because everything he did was just behavioral. Turns out, he's been here for seven months! Can you imagine living in the ER for seven months? I think I might try to kill myself, too! I heard Maria telling the dayshift nurses that his mom had come to see him only once since he has been here.

The sad thing is she is still his legal guardian. She won't give it up. Like Misty, I'm sure she gets a check for him every month. Honestly, it would be the best thing for him if she did simply sign him over to DSS. The nurses talked about working with him on his anger management and how much progress he had made in the time he was here. Maria even said that she had started taking the certification classes so that she could begin fostering kids like him. I heard her say that all the kids that came through here just needed a home with love and structure and most of us could be saved. I think she may be right.

I don't know how close he came to being successful in his attempt the other day, but he certainly left a big impression on everyone.

———

This afternoon there was an overhead page for security for a disturbance in the ambulance bay. Maria jumped up and yelled for everyone to get ready. The nurses and techs all moved to one of the empty rooms. It is amazing to watch them. There were four of them getting restraints attached to the bed while another one was at a cart gathering the supplies they would need when the patient came in. Another one ran to the med room - I found out later they did a manual override to get medication to calm what turned out to be a very highly combative patient.

It looked like there were fifteen people on top of this guy they were bringing in. He had EMS, police, and security on him. He was being held down, but he was fighting it. Maria got the syringe and made sure that he was held down, then she gave him the shot.

He started to slow down pretty fast. I could see the muscles in his neck and jaw start unclenching and his breathing started to deepen. One by one the security guards and police officers let go of him. None of them moved very far away - I'm pretty sure they didn't trust him to completely relax.

Maria looked at one of the officers and said, "Okay, now Quenton, you are going to have to tell me what the hell was that? We have had Jacquez in here many times and he has never behaved like this!"

The officer was wiping a whole lot of sweat off of his face and said, "Well, I'll tell you, Maria. His Mama decided that she is going on vacation with her flavor of the month. The last time we brought him in was, what, six months ago? When Mama had that flavor of the month buy her a buttjob?"

Maria made a face and said, "Yes, I remember."

"Well, Mama is going on vacation, a cruise I think she said, with, get this, a new baby daddy."

"No!"

One of the medics said, "Oh, yeah. Mama is pregnant and she and the new baby daddy are going on a cruise for a few weeks. Jacquez was mad when we got to the house, but lost it when the new boyfriend said that he wasn't sure if there was going to be room for Jacquez in the new home they are buying when they return. Jacquez told him to shut up. The guy puffed up his chest and said bring it. Jacquez threw the first punch. We called for the police when the two of them started tearing the house apart."

During the time they were talking, the nurses and the techs had gotten the now sleeping patient from the EMS gurney onto one of the ER beds. He didn't wake up when they moved him. He didn't wake up when they changed him. He didn't even wake up when they took blood from him! As tall as he was, I thought he was a grown man. I mean, he is really tall!

Turns out, he's only a sixteen-year-old kid!

October 23

I was awake before shift change this morning. Maria came in - I had no idea how early she starts her day. I'm pretty sure she got here at six and talked to the night shift supervisor about everything that had happened overnight.

Jacquez slept all night. I would have known that even if I hadn't been eavesdropping on their conversation. Once he got that shot, he was done. I hope he didn't have to pee overnight.

Maria came over to my room when she was finished talking to the nightshift nurse and asked me how I'd slept, if I had any pain anywhere. Pretty much all the same stuff that everyone else asked me everyday.

No, I don't want to hurt myself or anyone else. I am not feeling violent in any way, shape or form. No, I don't want to go to sleep and not wake up, or just die. I want to live - just not here! And, no, I don't see or hear things that aren't really there. But, if that really were my reality, how would I know they weren't there? I mean, they would seem real to me, wouldn't they?

After she asked me about seeing or hearing things that weren't there, I asked her, "How would I know?"

She said, "Excuse me?"

I asked, "How would I know if what I was seeing or hearing wasn't real? I mean, are you real? And if you weren't would you be able to tell me you weren't real? Is this all a dream or delusion?"

Maria shook her head and said, "Hey, kid, it's way too early in the morning to be getting this philosophical with me. I haven't even had my first cup of coffee or Celsius yet."

"Is Jacquez going to be okay?"

Maria brought me into my room and told the sitter to take a break. "You know I can't talk to you about another patient. It would violate HIPAA. Just know that he is stable."

"Oh, I know that. I mean, he slept through the night, and all. I just mean, what about his family. It sounds horrible! His mother sounds….Why do people even bother having kids? I mean, if you don't want a kid, don't have one. Or give it up for adoption right away so that it has a fighting chance." I was working myself up into crying for what seemed like the millionth time in the last few weeks.

Maria sat down on the bed next to me, put her arms around me and pulled me in close so that I could cry on her shoulder. "Hey, I can't guarantee anything other than that we will take care of you while you are here. We are working very closely with social services and our case management team to find you a good placement. You just remember this: You are a good kid! And you are so smart. Don't you ever let anyone try to take that away from you. You are a survivor and you will survive this. I believe in you."

I wrapped my arms around her and cried into her shoulder. When I had exhausted myself from the tears I looked at Maria and said, "Thank you. There has only been one other person in my life who has said they believed in me."

Maria asked, "Who was that?"

"Mrs. M."

———

I took a nap after Maria left my room. When I woke up I saw that Jacquez had visitors. It looked like maybe a grandmother and another lady. He was smiling and talking to them about how he planned to behave better and he would try not to fight with his mom's boyfriend. He asked the grandmother if he could go home with her today. She dropped her head and gave a small shake.

Jacquez lost his smile and looked deflated.

Just a few minutes later both ladies left. As soon as the doors closed behind them, there were loud pounding sounds coming from his room. Maria, another nurse and one of the techs ran to him. Maria told him to stop punching the wall, then I heard a scream that sounded like a wild animal in pain. Several security officers ran toward the door, but Maria yelled out to them, "We're fine. We don't need any help."

I walked to my door so I could look into his room. My sitter told me a couple of times that I should probably step further back into my room, that I didn't need to be in the doorway. I sat down on the floor instead. I thought it might be considered a compromise. I really just wanted to see what was going on with Jacquez.

All three women were holding him. It was pretty amazing, actually. All three of these ladies, holding onto this huge beast of a boy, comforting and consoling him while he cried. The sounds coming from his room made me want to cry with him. I can only describe it as the sound of a heart being shattered. Once a heart is that badly mangled is it possible to fit the pieces back together again?

I watched for close to an hour while Jacquez buried his head in Maria's shoulder and wept. The other nurse sat on the bed behind him rubbing his back and speaking to him softly. The tech sat beside him gently stroking his arm and occasionally sweeping his hair back from his face. The one thing all three women had in common? They were all crying with him.

—

Maria was the last to leave his room. She returned to the nurses' station and slumped into her chair looking defeated. She told one of the other nurses, "I can't do this anymore. These kids...I just can't. What the hell is wrong with people? I mean, these are good kids and these adults have just thrown them away! My God! If I could, I would take them all home with me."

The other nurse sitting with her said, "Maria, I think you

need a break."

"No, what I need is for someone to have some fucking accountability. I need to know who to contact to get these kids into homes where they will be loved and treated like human beings!" Her voice was thick, and I could tell she was close to tears. "These kids deserve to be loved. They need…" Her voice cracked as she put her face in her hands and broke down. Through her tears she said, "They deserve so much better than this."

I spent the rest of the day thinking about what it took for someone like Maria, who has seen so much in the emergency room, to completely lose her composure over kids like me.

October 24

Maria came in this morning looking like she was on a mission. She told the other nurses that she had a bunch of calls to make and if they needed her, just to let her know between calls.

The last few days had been so full of drama for me, I chose to turn on the TV and watch movies. One of my favorites has always been "27 Dresses." While surfing through the TV channels, I found that one playing and kept watching. I think my favorite part of the movie is when Katherine Heigl and that really hot guy from X-Men sing "Bennie and the Jetts" by Elton John in the bar.

The movie had just gotten to that part when I heard Maria raising her voice on the phone. "No, I want to speak with a supervisor."

I turned down the volume on my TV and scooted back in bed so I was hidden by the doorway.

"Yes, ma'am. My name is Maria Holden. I am the nurse manager for the emergency department here and I need to set up an appointment to discuss the lack of progress on the placement of three of the patients in my unit."

She paused and took notes on what the person on the phone was saying. She had half a page covered before she started speaking again. "Yes, I am aware that this is something typically handled by case management or a social worker. I have one child who has been waiting here for seven months and we are starting to collect more children. There has to be a better solution than for them to stay in what amounts to a twelve by twelve cell. They are children, not inmates."

I spent the rest of this afternoon splitting my attention between watching romantic comedies and watching and listening to Maria make phone call after phone call in an effort to get someone to take us. I listened to her work through a wide range of different emotions, and varying levels of anger and frustration. The last phone call that she made before calling it quits for the day, ended with her throwing her pen across the emergency room and yelling, "Damn it!"

My nurse for the day, I can't remember her name, asked Maria what was wrong.

Maria blew out a breath and leaned back in her chair with her fingers interlaced and her hands resting on top of her head. She said, "I just feel like I'm spinning my wheels. These kids deserve so much more than hospital scrubs, a jail cell sized room, and no stability. We don't have the resources to be their nurses, teachers, parents, and social workers."

The other nurse asked, "What's the answer, then? It's not

like we can turn them away. At least while they're here they're safe, clean, have a bed and three meals a day. Not all kids out there have that."

Maria said, "I know. I know that it's unrealistic of me to think that I can save all of them. This one over here doesn't have anyone. She had a family who wanted her, but that fell through when she got into a fight. From everything I've been able to read, the family didn't want to terminate their foster status, but the legal guardian stepped in and pulled her. A legal guardian, who by the way cannot be reached by phone. Jacquez has a family, but his mom is just a horrible human being. I can't even begin to imagine choosing some low life male scum over my own child. What in the hell is she thinking? I mean, he is one of the sweetest kids you will ever meet, but she's never given him a chance to succeed!"

"Maria…"

"No, I am pissed off! This is not fair to any of us – least of all these kids. I feel like forced sterilization should be a requirement if you consistently make bad choice. Or if any of your children are born addicted to anything."

At that point, I couldn't keep quiet. I said, "If all people who made bad choices were forced to be sterilized you never would have had the pleasure of meeting me. My mom started doing drugs at fourteen and had me at sixteen."

Maria jumped up and ran to my room. "I am so sorry. None of that was meant for you to hear. It has been a bad couple of days for me and I have been shooting off at the mouth. I know that is no excuse, but sometimes I have no filter."

I told her, "It's okay. I think a lot about stuff like that. I believe that if people create a baby and don't really want it, they should go ahead and give the baby up as soon as it's born, have a plan for adoption. I also believe that any parent who gives birth to a baby who is addicted to drugs should automatically give up their rights to that baby. Those are the ones I want to have to have forced sterilization.

"I think that people who want to foster kids need to be investigated a lot more than they actually are. Once the kids are in their homes, social workers should do random visits that way they can see what's really going on. I also think foster parents need to have special training to deal with kids who have had a lot of trauma, which, face it, would be most of us in the foster care system."

When I stopped talking, both Maria and the other nurse, I should probably learn her name, were staring at me.

"What," I asked.

Maria said, "You should do presentations for social services about fostering and adoption."

I snorted. "Yeah, like anyone really wants to hear what I have to say."

"No, I'm not kidding. I think that it would be a great idea for you to get up and speak at training events for social services. People need to hear what life is like for kids in the system. Aside from those of us who work with you kids, no one really understands what you experience."

I could feel my stomach dropping. "I don't think I could speak in front of an audience like that."

"Why not," Maria asked. "You had no problem speaking up just now. What if you were to start with our case management staff? There are only two or three on duty at any time. You could talk to them about what you think kids need."

"Why me," I asked. "There's nothing special about me."

Maria came over to me and hugged me and said, "You have no idea just how special you are."

October 24

It was sunny and nice outside today so Jason, Jacquez and I all went outside for a while. The hospital has an enclosed courtyard area for the patients like us who are simply problem children. The courtyard has a basketball hoop, a picnic table with benches, a locker that has a variety of "safe" outdoor toys and sidewalk chalk, and a large grassy area. Of course there is a huge fence surrounding the courtyard so we are still locked up, but it gives us a chance to go outside and get fresh air. Lavender was planted all along the fence line, so there is this wonderful fragrance all through the yard. When the breeze picks up and it's warm out, it feels like a great big lavender hug.

The boys immediately grabbed a basketball and started a game of one on one. I went to the far side of the yard and lay down on the grass right next to the lavender. I wanted to feel the sun on my skin, close my eyes and smell the lavender mixed with the warm salty air. The combination is so very relaxing. I love being able to be outside.

I love times like this. No one is talking to me. I can hear the distinct rubbery smack sound of the basketball hitting the blacktop. The boys are laughing and sound almost carefree. I can hear a bird close by chirping out its little song. For the first time in a long time, I'm relaxed.

I'm pretty sure I was so relaxed that I fell asleep at one point. Going outside is a bit of an ordeal. There is a lot of coordination involved, so there's never any guarantee that we will be able to on any given day. There have to be enough techs working on that day and there has to be a security guard available when we want to go out. It's the same thing with showers. None of us have showers in our rooms, so we have to wait until there are people available to take us to another section of the emergency department to shower.

The other day Jason, who came back to our little slice of Heaven after his wrist was sewn up, missed his chance to shower and threw a huge temper tantrum because he couldn't go when he wanted to. I wanted to tell him he was being an idiot. They tell us first thing in the morning, that they have enough staff right then, and we should go when we have the chance. I figure I can always sleep later in the day – I'll get up early for a shower.

When we came back inside I found a large paper shopping bag on my bed. I asked my sitter if she knew where it came from. She looked kind of bored and said, "Nope," she hadn't been sitting there the whole time I was outside, so she had no idea where it came from. Maria wasn't around and neither was my nurse – I found out her name is Erica. I wanted to open the bag, but thought it had to have been brought to my room by mistake.

I sat on my bed and waited for one of the nurses to come back by. The sitter asked me if I wanted to open the bag. I told her I wasn't even sure if it was mine so I thought I'd better wait. Maria came rushing into the unit after I'd been waiting about ten minutes. I have discovered something about Maria – she doesn't do anything slowly. Everything is full speed ahead and get out of the way, or you will be steamrolled. It's not a bad thing. She gets things done!

She came barreling into my room and asked me if I was planning on opening the bag.

"Where did it come from," I asked.

"A couple of the nurses and I got together and we got a few things for you and the boys."

I could feel the burning of the start of tears in my eyes, and my throat felt thick. I don't think that I have ever had a group of nurses try to love me. These women were incredible! I can't speak for the boys, but it makes me feel special to know that they really care. I had no idea how to respond other than to drop my eyes and open the bag. All I can say is it felt like what I think Christmas is supposed to feel like.

The bag was full to the top with clothes and shower stuff. The nurses had been paying attention when I went outside. They knew that I loved the lavender in the courtyard and I had talked about Mrs. M's herb garden. They got me lavender mint shampoo and conditioner. There was a lavender eucalyptus blend body wash, and a variety of different body lotions. There was also a pink shower caddy for me to carry my things to the shower.

In addition to the shower stuff, there was clothing. There were leggings and T-shirts in pinks, purples, silver and gold and two sweatshirts for when it starts to get cold out. There were also underpants, socks, and slip-on shoes. They also bought me a pair of pajamas that were white with pink trim with Dumbo all over them. At the very bottom of the bag were two books and a stuffed black lab. The one book was *The Secret Garden*. The other was one I had never read before: *Miss Peregrine's Home for Peculiar Children*.

I pulled the stuffed dog out of the bag last. It looked so much like Koda, I almost started crying. It even had a little collar with a tag that had the name Koda on it. I climbed up on the bed cradling my new stuffed dog and looked at all my new clothes and my books. To be honest, it was kind of overwhelming. I'm not used to people celebrating me. All of the clothes were brand new. Not Goodwill new, but actually brand new.

Maria and Erica watched from the doorway. I think they were giving me space to deal with all my swirling emotions.

"Hey, sweetheart," Maria said. "Do you think those clothes are going to fit?"

"Yes. Thank you so much. All of you." My voice cracked as I spoke, and I could feel the sting of tears in my eyes. Maria and Erica both came over and hugged me.

Maria said, "Most of this was because of Erica."

Erica shrugged and said, "I was just thinking that my little girls would hate not having pretty clothes to wear, and no one enjoys wearing these ugly hospital scrubs. They helped me pick out everything, even the shampoo and body wash."

"I love the scents. How did you know about Koda?"

Erica smiled and said, "We listen. Sometimes when you are outside or when you talk with the techs you mention Koda and you talk about everything you loved when you were with the McClellands. We couldn't bring you Koda, but we thought that having this little guy might brighten your spirits."

Tears spilled over and went streaking down my face. I couldn't hold it in anymore. There are times when my emotions feel so much bigger than I am. I don't really know how to describe them. I don't have the right words for them. These nurses have been nicer to me than most of the foster parents I have ever had. They've been nicer to me than my own grandmother ever was. And I know that there will come a point when I am placed with yet another family and I will probably never see any of them again.

"Oh, sweetheart, we were hoping this would make you happy." Maria looked like she was about to cry, too.

I sniffled and cried. "I am happy. I have never mattered to anyone before. No one has ever tried to take care of me. It feels good, but it also scares the shit out of me. What happens after this? Where am I going to go? I don't want to live here in the emergency room, but I also don't want to go back to another awful foster home or group home. It just feels nice to be able to sort of be a kid and let someone else care for me. The only other time I have ever felt loved was when I was with Mr. and Mrs. M."

When I finished talking, I buried my head in Koda and ugly cried. I think it was okay though because I'm pretty sure Maria, Erica and the sitter were crying with me.

—

OH MY GOSH!!! I just had the best shower ever!! After all of us finished our ugly crying session, I told Maria and Erica that I needed a shower. I really wanted to wash off the sweat from having been outside, but I also needed to kind of wash away all the emotion of the day. I washed my hair yesterday, but I had to try the shampoo and conditioner. IT WAS AWESOME!!! The combined scents of lavender and mint filled the steamy bathroom. It was so relaxing! When I added the lavender eucalyptus body wash, the shower smelled like Heaven to me.

After spending entirely too much time under the hot water, I dried off, wrapped my hair in a towel and put on my Dumbo pajamas. The security officer and the tech walked me back to my room where I settled in my bed and combed out my hair. Once all the knots had been worked out, I got under the covers with my stuffed Koda and *The Secret Garden*. For just a few minutes, I was able to pretend that I was home with the Mc-Clellands. If I close my eyes, I can imagine the green room with the twin beds. Cadence would be in the next bed over. I would be reading with my reading lamp on while she would pull her sleep mask over her eyes so my light wouldn't bother her.

There were a lot of times when I would turn off the light and we would start talking and giggling. I loved having someone to talk to at the end of the day. Someone who got me. Cadence would tell me secrets, like which boy at school she liked, but was too shy to talk to. She even told me once that when she had first gone to live with Mr. and Mrs. M she had a really huge crush on Erik. I could understand that, too. He's cute and really nice. She told me that after she had lived there for a little while, she came to look at him too much like a brother. She told me that even though she used to have a crush on him, she loves that he is her big brother.

October 25

I fell asleep last night snuggled with my stuffed Koda. When I closed my eyes to imagine being back in the green room with Cadence, I ended up falling asleep. I think I'm going to start imagining life back on the farm right before I go to bed now. Last night was one of the best nights of sleep I've had since I was taken away. I dreamed about the McClellands rescuing me from the hospital. They brought me home and adopted me. That would be a dream come true!

The last few days here on the unit have been pretty quiet. That changed sometime around mid-morning. I was reading my book and curled up with Koda when security started moving fast. I heard something about a combative patient over one of the guards' radios. Erica went running to the supply room and grabbed restraints, one of the techs ran to a supply cart and started pulling the supplies that they take to every new patient. Maria went to the room to make sure it was ready and grabbed the machine they use to take vital signs.

I could hear them coming long before they got to the unit. The doors swung open and security and the police came in with EMS and a man who was strapped down on the stretcher and screaming.

"GET THEM OFF! GET THEM OFF!" He was straining against the restraints and digging into his hands with his fingernails.

The EMS lady pushing his stretcher said to him, "Sweetie, there's nothing on you." She brought the patient to a room and told Erica, "He has been screaming about things crawling on him and biting him the whole ride. We had to fight him to get him onto the stretcher."

Erica asked, "Does he have bedbugs?"

The lady from EMS said, "We didn't see any evidence of bedbugs, but I do think he was attacked by some of them methsquitos coming up off the Cape Fear. Anyway, this is Robert Carter, twenty-nine year old male. Police called us out to the Circle K on Market Street because, well, he was acting like this. He was pulling out his hair in clumps, clawing at his face. At one point he started to dig at his eyes. That's when we went for the restraints. He has been fighting the restraints the whole way.

"We tried to start a line on him, but that didn't work. We ended up giving him two milligrams of Versed, and as you can see, that didn't touch him at all."

While she was talking, the guy was in the background yelling about bugs crawling around inside his eyes and that they were biting his brain. I heard a loud crash and a scream and then the guy was at the door to my room. I had no idea where the sitter was.

The guy was talking out of his head. "You know where they are, don't you?"

He was coming right toward me, and I was terrified.

"Why are you following me? You put something in my water again, didn't you? When I get my hands on you, I'm going to KILL YOU!"

I managed to jump off the bed, get the wheels unlocked and pull it diagonally into the corner so that it blocked me from him and I curled into as small of a ball as I could behind the stretcher.

"Where the fuck did you go, you little bitch? You need to come out…"

I heard a lot of movement and then he was facedown on my bed looking over the side at me.

"There are you," he said. His voice was almost loving, like he had found something precious. It didn't match the look of pure hatred on his face, which was half covered by his long, greasy hair. As close as his face was to mine I could see scabs from where he had tried to pick at the bugs he thought were crawling through his skin. I could also see that what he had left of his teeth were in various stages of blackening. All of them looked rotten, and the smell coming from his mouth made me think that most of his insides were pretty rotten, too.

"GET OFF ME YOU FUCKING PIG!!" He was shouting

at the police and security officers who were trying to wrestle him off my bed and back to his room, which happened to be right next to mine.

"Ow! Something just bit my ass! What the fuck just bit my ass?"

"Mr. Carter," Maria's voice said. "I have just given you a shot of Geodon to help you calm down."

"FUCK YOU, BITCH! I AM GOING TO SUE THIS EN-TIRE HOSPITAL." Another stretcher was wheeled into my room and the guards and officers fought him off of my bed and onto the stretcher. While they held him down, there was so much commotion. I peeked up over the side of the bed to see if I could see anything. I swear it looked like there were ten people on him. There was either a nurse or tech at each one of his limbs, four security guards and I recognized Officer Burns helping keep him held down. The man screamed and yelled the entire time.

Once he was securely restrained and back in his room I heard Maria in the hallway.

"Where the hell is the sitter for this room? Who was here, Christina? Where is she? Where is Storm?"

I answered her from behind the bed, "I'm in here."

Officer Burns came in and said, "Hey, Storm. How about we get you some clean sheets? You don't want to get back in bed after that guy's been rolling around in it."

I said, "Okay" and I let him lead me out of the room.

"Do you want to go outside for a bit," he asked.

I just nodded. He asked Maria if it would be ok for him and one of the security officers to take me and the other kids out. She said it was fine and sent one of the techs with us.

—

We stayed outside for close to an hour. I think everyone needed the decompression time. Officer Burns asked me several times if I was okay while we were out there. He really is very nice. Because of him I am starting to appreciate police officers a lot more than I ever did in the past. Because they only ever showed up when things were at their absolute worst, I always associated them with the bad stuff. It never occurred to me before that they were there to help. Of course firefighters usually only show up when things are pretty bad and everyone loves them. Go figure!

Amazingly, it was silent as a tomb when we got back to our little area. The screaming crazy guy finally got enough meds into him to knock him out, which is good because he was really scary. Also, when I got back to my room, Christina, my sitter had miraculously reappeared. I found out later that when the crazy guy started barreling down the hall to my room, Christina jumped up, ran through the nurses' station and left the department.

Now, I know that the sitters are only there to sound the alarm should I try to run, but really? Some methed out guy was running toward the room where a kid was, and the adult ran away? I'm kind of disappointed in her as an adult.

The nurses here are kind of badass. I mean, here is this guy fighting with everyone and these women - who by the way, are all small women - are jumping right into the middle of it with the guards and the officers. Christina might be a dud, but I know that I am safe with the rest of the adults around me.

October 26

We got another kid on the unit today. I'm pretty sure that Maria is about to lose her mind because of all the kids on the unit. I heard her on the phone arguing with someone from social services saying that this is not a safe or appropriate place for children to be raised. I can't say I disagree. I don't want to grow up here.

The kid that came in today is Antoine. He is another really tall kid, and I think he and Jacquez know each other either from another hospital stay or from a group home. Antoine was wheeled in wearing handcuffs and a spit hood. The officers who brough him in told Maria the hood was necessary because he wouldn't stop spitting at them.

The spit hood looks sort of like a mesh bag on the top where the eyes and the top of the head are. The bottom sort of looks like a chef's hat. The smooth part of the hat that goes on the forehead is down around the throat, while the big puffy part goes over the mouth so when the person spits, it gets caught in the fabric.

I could see through the mesh of the hood that he was bleeding from the nose and mouth. Maria interrogated the officers asking how that had happened. I'm pretty sure she scared the crap out of them - she can be pretty scary sometimes. She is fiercely protective of her staff and her patients - even the ones that come in acting like assholes.

Antoine was brought in because he was beating the crap out of his foster mom. He has lived with her for two weeks and she wouldn't let him have chicken tenders for lunch. That was it, no chicken tenders for lunch. She wanted him to eat something healthy. I heard the officer say that foster mom came into the hospital by ambulance and she was the patient who went into the trauma room. Maria asked why Antoine was brought here and not taken to jail. The officer said it was because he was only fifteen.

I want to know what it is that they are feeding these boys here in Wilmington. Jacquez is sixteen and well over six feet tall, Antoine is only fourteen and he is as tall as Jacquez, but built even bigger. He looks like he should be playing football. That might actually help him get out some of his aggression.

Maria asked him if he was going to give her any trouble and he just shook his head. After they did all of the stuff to get him ready for the unit, one of the techs asked him if he wanted anything. He asked her if they had any stuffed animals or teddy bears that he could sleep with. He told her that he was afraid of the dark and needed a stuffed animal to protect him. I would have thought he was five or six from the way he talked. Could it be possible that we're all a little messed up?

I'm not really sure what the hospital is going to do if they get many more of us kids. No one seems to want us. Social services can't find appropriate placements and we are taking up beds. This ER has a total of twelve beds for emergency behavioral health patients. Right now, us throwaway kids are taking up four of those beds.

October 27

Today was probably the grossest day of my life. Erica had a patient come in who had overdosed on fentanyl. Someone gave him Narcan before he got here and it produced a literal shitstorm. When EMS got him into his room, he leaned over the side of his stretcher and threw up on the floor. Erica went in with a towel to start cleaning and he messed himself. Since they always change out the psych patients anyway, Erica went ahead and started to change him. She ran to the supply room to grab wipes, a basin, some soap, towels and washcloths so she could start to clean him.

As soon as Erica got back to the room, the real show began. The patient had stripped himself because he wanted to get the nasty mess away from his body. He had been complaining about stomach cramps, so he had curled himself into the fetal position on the bed. I walked by his door on my way to the bathroom as he screamed in pain and pulled his knees closer to his chest, causing an explosive rush of diarrhea to shoot from him across the room and into the hallway.

I gagged because of the smell then I sprinted to the bathroom. One of the security guards threw up in the room and then left the unit. Erica ran to the supply room to grab more towels. There was another security guard who went into the room to help Erica with the clean up. Every time either Erica or the guard came out of the room for more cleaning supplies, they would gag, but they kept going back.

The smell...oh, dear God the smell! I'm not sure how to begin to describe it. All I can say is that it was unlike anything I had ever experienced before. One of the security guards said it smelled like pure evil had touched our unit, and that was not the last of the explosive episodes. At one point, the guy was on all fours on top of the stretcher and it was shooting out of him. When I say it was "shooting" out of him, it was hitting the wall on the opposite side of the hall! Erica and the guard were right there the whole time. As soon as they got one mess cleaned up, the guy exploded again. At the end of all of it, I found out that Erica had just gotten brand new white shoes. Well, they started the shift white, anyway. Seeing that today makes me never want to be a nurse. I don't know how they do it!

October 28

Jason went home this morning. I don't know if it was for real home, but he was at least picked up and taken away from here. I'm happy for him, but I'd be lying if I said it didn't bother me. I don't want to be here anymore. As nice as these nurses have been to me, and as great as they've taken care of me, I just want to have a forever home. At the very least, a get out of the hospital home.

I would love to be able to say that whatever placement I get I will stay there and behave as best as I can, but I know that's probably not going to happen, especially if it's a place with someone like Misty. I have to keep telling myself that I'm happy for Jason, but I'm really jealous.

To be honest, I haven't been here all that long, not even ten days, but I am so tired of living in a hospital.

October 29

Today is the tenth day that I've been in the hospital. All I have wanted to do is curl up with my stuffed Koda and sleep. Maria and Erica have been trying to get me up and moving, but what's the point? It's not like I can leave my room. I don't want to get up, I don't want to eat, I don't want to shower. I just want to stay curled up with my Koda bear and either cry or sleep. I don't even want to read or watch TV. I would love it if they would just give me some Zyprexa and leave me alone. The perfect escape would be into a faraway dreamworld. If I get motivated enough later, maybe I can write my own little fantasy world.

I could write a story that starts with once upon a time and takes place in an enchanted forest. Maybe in my enchanted forest, I will encounter a magical, talking unicorn who will let me ride on her. As we gallop through the trees, she will sprout iridescent wings and we can take off in flight. She would fly me over vast stretches of water to a remote castle that stands at the top of a cliff. When we landed, there would be crowds of people waiting to get a glimpse of the beautiful, exotic princess about to be crowned queen of all the land.

The way my brain works, I will create this wonderful fantasy world right before I go to sleep, then I'll end up dreaming about getting high in a meth house that has no electricity or running water.

Maybe if I start to act out badly enough I can get them to restrain and medicate me. It's not like any of them have any plans to take me home anyway. God, sometimes I really do wish that I could go to sleep and never wake up. Living in a dream world is almost always so much better than the real world.

October 30

I don't even have the energy to try to pitch a fit. I woke up this morning and discovered that while I was sleeping yesterday both Antoine and Jacquez went home. I'm sure there will be other kids who cycle in and out of here, but I feel like I'm stuck. Maybe I can start asking for medicine to help me with anxiety and just hoard it all. That way I can take it and just go to sleep.

It hurts so much to know that there is no one out there who wants me. I can't do this anymore.

October 31

At some point over the last few days, the unit has cleared out and I am the only patient left. Even the crazy adult patients have been discharged. I walked out of my room this morning to use the bathroom and walked into a Halloween wonderland. There were fake cobwebs hung everywhere! Inside the cobwebs were plastic spiders. On the corners of each of the room doors, the nurses had hung bats. There were also rubber bats hanging from some of the ceiling tiles.

There were large stuffed owls sitting on top of the supply carts, and stuffed black cats scattered around the unit. They had put out black and orange electric flickering candles. On several different workspace surfaces they had put out Jack-o-lanterns with small battery-operated tea light candles. They really went all out decorating! The best touch was the full sized skeleton wearing a security guard costume propped in one of the chairs. They even had a costume for me – Wednesday Addams!

I'm pretty sure I actually squealed when they gave me the costume to change into. I ran down the hallway to the bathroom, tore off my T-shirt and leggings as fast as I could and put on the costume. It was a simple black dress that buttoned down the front with a stiff white collar. There were black stockings and black shoes to go with it. Erica helped me with my hair, parting it perfectly down the middle and braiding both sides. When my hair was all done, Maria gave me the finishing touch - a fake hand that could sit on my shoulder to act as Thing. Coolest costume ever!!!

I came out of my room and showed off my costume to the sitters who all told me how great the costume was. Maria handed me a pumpkin shaped bucket and told me it was time to go trick or treating. Now, I've seen the whole trick or treat thing done on TV and in movies, but I've never actually done it. Grandma used to say that celebrating Halloween was just inviting Satan to take up residence in your soul. As uptight as she was, she would have looked at trick or treating as begging the neighbors for food – also taboo. I'm pretty sure if she knew I was dressed as Wednesday Addams, she'd hire an exorcist for me and pray for the souls of the hospital staff for giving me the costume.

When I shared that thought with Maria, she laughed so hard, she snorted and had to wipe tears from her eyes. Maria told me that we were going to go trick or treating a little differently - I was going to follow clues and go to different units throughout the hospital. Each unit would have a different candy reward. Once I got to the last unit, I would have a big surprise. I told her it really didn't matter what method we used since I'd never been before.

I said, "Let's go!" I wasn't entirely sure about the whole scavenger hunt thing, but I was very excited about actually leaving the unit, wearing real clothes and the possibility of getting candy out of the deal. So I have to use my brain to figure out where I'm going first, how horrible would that be?

The first card read, *Your patient has been in a car accident that required firefighters to use the jaws of life to get them out. What is their first stop?*

I looked at Maria and said, "Well, duh! They're going to go to the emergency room!"

She said, "Okay, smarty pants. But what part of the emergency room? You have been living in the emergency room for the last few days. Where would someone be taken if they had been injured in a car accident?"

I stopped walking and really had to think about it. As I was thinking, an overhead page went out. "Trauma alert, room one. Trauma alert, room one."

"Oh! The trauma room!"

Maria grinned and said, "I will lead the way."

"You're actually going to let me watch a trauma code?"

Maria said, "Oh, no. We're going to go to the nurses' station right outside of trauma room one. You won't be able to see anything, but the nurses there have your next clue and the candy prize."

We got to the station right outside of the trauma room and the nurse gave me a handful of chocolate. I think it was mostly bite sized butterfingers, which are one of my favorites! She talked to me a little bit about what they do in trauma situations and showed me one of the empty trauma rooms. It was really cool! It's almost like they've condensed the entire ER supply room into one room. They are bigger than the regular ER rooms, but that makes sense since there are usually more people working in a trauma situation and they need different equipment than they would need in a regular room.

I think Maria figured out that I love learning stuff, so this is her way of letting me get exposed to more science-y things. I am definitely not complaining.

The next clue read, *Just like Superman, we can see right through you, unless you're wearing lead.*

I yelled, "X-ray!"

We went over to Radiology and they showed me some of the coolest images! I got to see images of broken bones. One of the techs over there showed me how they can look at images and see when people have pneumonia or lung cancer, and how they can even see when people have super brittle bones. They can even find stuff in people like blockages when they are really constipated or, the grossest thing, when there is stuff shoved up there that shouldn't be there. One picture he showed me was after a guy fell at a construction site. He had been on scaffolding, lost his balance and fell onto some rebar. This one piece of rebar somehow entered him in between his collar bones and angled down. It missed his heart, but got one of his lungs and his liver and came out his side. The tech said the guy was messed up for a while, but he ended up living.

—

All in all, we ended up visiting twelve different departments. In each department, I got to see and learn about different things. I think my favorite was the NICU. It could be because that was my first home, but I think, honestly, it's because I looked at those tiny babies and knew each one of them was a tough little fighter. At that stage of life, you don't know that you aren't supposed to be able to live. No one has told you yet that you aren't good enough, you aren't loved enough or even wanted, or that you are damaged beyond all repair. Those little ones fight tougher battles just to survive one day after the next than most adults will ever realize. Most of the babies that were in the unit I visited were about the size of a twenty ounce soda bottle.

The NICU was where I got my final clue card. It simply read, *It's time to go back*. I told Maria that all of the other cards at least made me have to think. This clue was pretty lame, all things considered.

Maria said, "Yeah, I hear you, kiddo. But to be fair, my caffeine buzz had worn off. My clever well had run dry by the time I got to the twelfth clue, so it is what it is."

I jabbered on the whole way back to our unit. This was a lot of fun! It took my mind off the fact that the boys had all left and I when they came, I would be stuck with the crazy adults until a new placement came through. I figured, you know, Maria, Erica, and the other nurses are pretty cool. If I have to live here in the ER for a while, it isn't all that bad. I can ask my social worker to get me set up in online classes, maybe. I would love to start school again. Maybe they will let me study for my GED and I can start going to community college online. There are just so many thoughts. It's amazing how much this walk around the hospital has helped today!

We got to the unit door. Just before Maria could badge us through, I stopped her and gave her a big hug.

"What was that for," she asked.

"Thank you. Today has been so much fun. I didn't know what I was going to do if I had to sit in my room and just look at the wall again."

"Oh, sweetheart, you are so welcome! We know you've been so very depressed and we all wanted to help raise your spirits. It couldn't be easy watching the boys leave. I'm just happy you had fun today. I wasn't sure if the trick or treat slash science lesson was going to be fun for you."

"Are you kidding! Science is my favorite subject in school! I had a blast!"

She swiped us in and we walked onto the unit. There had been a lot of talking when the doors opened, but as soon as we walked in and they saw us everything went silent.

"What's going on," I asked. I can't explain it, but there was just this feeling. The nurses and the techs were all smiling like there was a big secret. The air on the unit felt like it had a charge to it, an electrical hum. Whatever it was, there was definitely a feeling in the air.

Maria, trying to suppress a smile said, "Why don't you head back to your room and we'll heat up your dinner tray for you."

I said, "Okay, but seriously is there something happening?"

Maria said, "Nope." Then she walked away.

I was muttering under my breath about how weird everyone was as I opened the door to my room. I turned on the light, looked at my bed, dropped my bucket of candy and just stood and stared.

Mr. and Mrs. M were sitting on my bed with big smiles on their faces.

———

I flew across the room and threw my arms around both of them. They hugged me back fiercely. I was crying hysterically and kept repeating over and over that I couldn't believe they found me. I asked probably a thousand times if this meant I could go home. They just kept hugging me and telling me it was okay. Everything was going to be okay.

About an hour later, Maria came in. Mr. M was doing his doctor thing and looking at my face. Examining me to make sure that I really was ok. Mrs. M made sure that she had one hand on me at all times. I can't really say much, I kept reaching out to make sure that I was touching at least one of them at all times, too. I was afraid that if I stopped, they would disappear.

I asked Maria how this was possible. She told me that she

and the hospital case workers had met with my case worker from social services on many occasions. They finally convinced her to reach out to the McClellands to find out if they would be willing to have me come back to live with them. When the McClellands said they would leave right away to come get me, the case worker cleared it with her supervisor and said that I was to be placed immediately in their care.

Mrs. M went one step further and asked that since there were no parental rights to terminate, would it be possible to start the application for adoption right away. The case worker said, "No" to that one, and that I would have to live with them for at least six months before they could petition for adoption. After that point they could petition for adoption and she had no doubt that the request would be approved.

I also found out that Mr. and Mrs. M have been searching for me since the day I was removed from their custody. Mrs. M told me she never stopped, that she would have kept looking for me for the rest of her life and was thrilled when Maria and the Granville County social services office were able to reach her and tell her where I was and that she would be able to bring me back home.

So, by eight o'clock on Halloween night, I was discharged from the hospital and was spending a quiet night in a hotel room with the two most amazing parents in the world!

November 1

Today was one of the best days of my life. Yesterday was amazing and I am so incredibly grateful to the nurses and the social workers who brought me back together with the only people I ever truly felt were my family. The eight of us just work. We fit together like we were all made as a set, only somehow the pieces got separated and lost for a while. I can't really explain it any other way.

We got up really early and checked out of the hotel. Mr. M wanted to get an early start since it is a six hour drive from Wilmington to Sylva. Those six hours felt like they both flew by and dragged at the same time. It felt like the hands of the clock were spinning while stuck in quicksand. That's weird, isn't it? I just couldn't wait to get home. I love that word - *home*. I was so excited to see Erik, Cadence, Chloe, Zoe, and Brian. My family! I know it isn't always going to be sunshine and pink ponies, but I feel like life is better when you know you have people who love you just for you and that you belong somewhere. Even when I am my worst self with them they still accept me. I've never had that anywhere else. This is what it feels like to feel safe.

When we pulled into the driveway, my five crazy siblings spilled out of the house and were surrounding the car before we were completely stopped. Erik opened my car door and pulled me out of the car to give me a huge bear hug. The rest of them swarmed us. Poor little Brian was jumping up and down hooting.

I interpreted his hoots to mean, "I want to hug her, too!"

I picked him up and tickled his side. He giggled. It was the sweetest sound I had heard in forever! As we were all loving each other, I heard a loud crash. I looked up to see my real Koda forcing open the screen door. He was across the yard and jumping on me, knocking me over, before I had a chance to put Brian back down. I guess even the animals missed me!

The six of us kids walked up to the house together. I turned back at one point to look at Mr. and Mrs. M and I saw them standing together each with an arm around the other, her head leaning on his shoulder. They wore matching smiles filled with total contentment.

One year later

It has been six months since my adoption was finalized and one whole year since mom and dad found me and brought me home. Mom and I have been asked to speak at this huge event supporting adoption and foster care. I have been told there is supposed to be a really large crowd of doctors, nurses, social workers and people who want to become foster or adoptive parents. Like I said, it's supposed to be a really big crowd.

I am a walking ball of nerves because I've never done any real public speaking – I don't feel like shooting off my mouth to Maria and Erica counts, but mom says it's really important for me to get my story out there. She says that people need to understand kids like me and understand that we aren't bad kids, we've just never been shown how to deal with the stuff that life throws at us. She also wants me to share my story because so few people know that when we misbehave, so many of us end up living in places like the emergency department, or sleeping in offices that were meant for social services workers.

Mom told me that while they were searching for me, she found an entire hospital unit dedicated to kids like me. It amazed me that there are so many throwaway kids out there.

I was surprised that Erik hadn't wanted to get up and share his story. When I asked him, he said that he would much rather let me step into the spotlight, that he would be cheering from the sidelines. When I asked Cadence why she didn't want to share her story, her already pale face lost even more color. She giggled nervously and said that she was fine, no one wanted to hear about her. Chloe and Zoe's adoption hasn't been finalized yet, and little Brian's biological parents still have legal rights to him. We are all hoping the adoption process can start soon for him!

—

The conference this afternoon was amazing! There was this whole thing about foster care and adoptive kids and some of the challenges that go along with raising them – especially if the kid has been moved around a lot. Mom was awesome! I don't know where to start! This whole experience has been, just, wow!

Okay, so I'll start with yesterday. We drove into Raleigh yesterday and we are staying in a really nice new hotel called Tempo. Mom got us this suite with a balcony that overlooks downtown Raleigh. There's also a rooftop restaurant where you can see for what feels like miles! It's such a cool experience. I don't think I'd ever want to live in Raleigh – it's too big, there are too many people, and I've really grown to love living in the mountains.

After we checked into the hotel, we walked around downtown for hours. We went to Nash Square which is this little park smack dab in the center of Raleigh. There was a guy there who told mom and me about how fortunate citizens of Raleigh were to have so much greenery in the downtown area. We both just smiled and kept walking. It's a cute park, but my backyard has a lot more greenery!

Mom has told me over and over again that this trip is about me, so anything I want to do, we're going to do it. After we walked through Nash Square, we walked over to see the state Capitol building. We walked by so many beautiful, historic churches along the way. We even walked over to the governor's mansion. There is so much to see! After we took the tour through the mansion, we were both feeling hungry and ready to settle in for the day. We went back to the hotel and ate dinner on the roof!

After dinner I took a long, hot bubble bath and then curled up on the king size bed with mom. My plan was to watch movies with her and pretend we were having a sleepover. I had *27 Dresses* and *Pretty in Pink* picked out. Mom teased me a little and said she didn't think I liked pink. I made a face at her and told her it was great as a movie title and a color, but was a stupid name! We giggled and snuggled in together. We put on *27 Dresses* first. I was asleep before Katherine Heigl's first wardrobe change.

—

Mom had this whole long speech that she prepared. She said that we are going to be a big part of changing the way the system works. I really hope so. I don't want any other child to have to go through what I have been through. Every kid deserves a forever family from the very start. We don't ask to be born.

The first time I got *toss my cookies* nervous was when I walked into the meeting room at the convention center. There were what looked like a thousand tables. I counted them later. There were thirty. Each table had ten chairs around it. Mom and I were among the first people to arrive. There were several tables at the front of the room that had name placards. We were seated at one of those tables. I was told it was because we were both speaking and we were the guests of honor.

Also at the front of the room was a small stage with a podium. The woman who had organized this event was a social worker for Wake County. I think she said she was a supervisor. Her name was Susan. There was so much that happened, I really can't remember everything.

Susan had us come up to the podium before other people arrived so we could put the notes we needed on the shelf on the inside. Mom had her laptop and they worked together to figure out how to get it set up so she could do her presentation. My presentation was just going to be me, my diary, and any other memories that came to me. When I told Susan, she said that would be enough.

About an hour after mom and I got there and were shown around, Susan opened the doors to the people who were attending. Wave after wave of people came crashing through and I was beginning to feel like I couldn't breathe! How was I going to tell my story in front of all of these people? And why was I so important, anyway? Mom must have felt me starting to tense up. She put her arm around me and pulled me into her. She grabbed my hand, gave it a squeeze as she whispered to me, "You are going to shine up there! Just be you!" Then she kissed me on the side of the head and tugged on my braid.

Susan took her place behind the podium and began, "Good afternoon, ladies and gentlemen. I want to welcome all of you. Our group today is composed of social workers, nurses, doctors, lawyers, law enforcement officers, foster parents, adoptive parents, future foster and adoptive parents, foster children, former foster children and adoptees. Today we are going to hear from and about the children we all work so very hard to protect. Whether you realize it or not, every one of you is in some way, a hero to at least one child. Every one of you has or will touch the life of a child and make a difference. The fact that you are here tells me that you want to be the one to change a child's life for the better.

"Some of the stories you are going to hear are going to be hard to listen to. Some of them are downright heartbreaking. I encourage you to ask questions when you can. Learn from today's speakers, they have a lot to share."

She went on to tell everyone that there was a buffet set up at the back of the room and to feel free to help themselves to food. She also said that they may want to start getting their food while she was talking because they weren't going to want to miss what was coming next. No pressure, right?

Susan talked on for another ten minutes while people throughout the room started filling their plates. The food smelled great, but there was no way I was going to be able to eat anything before I got up to speak.

She started to wrap things up and said, "Throughout the course of my career I have met many people who have truly valued our children and wanted to make a difference. I have never met anyone else like Ann McClelland and her husband. Robert couldn't be here with her today, so Ann will be speaking for both of them. The McClellands have fostered close to thirty children over the course of the last twenty years. The family has survived all the ups and downs that fostering can bring and they still open their hearts and home to children who need a home and the love of family. Please welcome Ann McClelland."

Mom walked up onto the stage. She looked so beautiful and seemed so calm. "Good afternoon. My name is Ann Mc-Clelland. My husband and I have been fostering children for much of the last twenty years. It is never an easy thing to bring someone else's children into your home and try to raise them, but we made it work because in the end, the children really are our future and it is so very important to try and repair the damage done by trauma.

"Many of you are starting on a new journey to foster. My advice is to give it time and be patient, especially with children who have either been very badly abused, or have had multiple disruptions in placement. These are the children who are going to push you to the limit to try to show you that they are completely unlovable. They will steal from you, run away in the middle of the night." Of course, she looked directly at me when she said this last one. "And they will lie to you and become destructive.

"I can see some of you out there rethinking your decision to start fostering. These behaviors are meant to test you. These children have been damaged and traumatized and they don't trust that you won't simply give up on them the first time they act out, so they start by acting out. They want so much for you to love them, but they don't trust that you will, so they purposely do everything they can to push you away. They are used to the adults in their lives bailing on them when things get tough."

A woman in the crowd asked, "How do you get them to trust you, then? How do you get to the point where you can trust them?"

Ann smiled, and said, "In some cases, you never win their trust and sometimes you can't trust them. Those are the hardest cases. I have had several children just like that. It broke my heart at the time, but after they left my care and moved into adulthood, they continued to come back to me for advice and love. My best advice is to be consistent and be real. These kids have a sixth sense about the adults in their lives and they know when you aren't being real.

"This is the absolute hardest job you will ever have, and trust me, it is a lot of work. To me and my husband, it was worth every second. For all of the horror stories, stop and think about this: You may be the only structure and stability this child has ever seen. Your love may be the only love the child you bring home has ever experienced. Is it worth it? Oh, yeah!

"I would not trade one broken window or stolen object for any of the children I have had the honor of fostering over the years. To me, those are just things. They can be replaced. The child that you bring home is a life that you may end up saving, a soul that needs to be rescued. Children are not replaceable."

I don't remember everything that mom said, but some of the stories she told about her experiences in fostering were both inspiring and heartbreaking. I had started thinking back on all my experiences in foster care and group homes. I am so happy that I never have to be a foster kid again. As I was thinking about how grateful I am to have my forever home, I heard mom wrapping up her portion of the talk.

"It now gives me great pleasure to have my daughter share some of her experiences with you."

There was a great deal of applause as mom waited for me on the stage. When I got to the podium, she gave me a huge hug, kissed me on the cheek and whispered to me, "You are going to be great, just take a deep breath, and be you."

I smiled and walked up to the microphone, which of course,

was too tall for me. It took a little bit of doing, and some help from Susan, but we adjusted everything so I could introduce myself.

"Hi, my name is Serenity McClelland. Many of you who have met me know me by the name Storm. I think it's safe to say that because of the love and patience mom and dad have given me, I have reached a point where I no longer feel the rage that used to fuel me. Storm is no longer appropriate.

"Mom talked to you about her experience as a foster care provider. What she didn't tell you is that through her years of fostering, she has always offered the possibility of adoption to each child who has come through their home. Which means, she has a lot of children!

"The point of my talk today is to impress upon all of you how important your role as a foster parent is. As a foster kid, many of us kind of blend into the background, no one sees us, no one hears us, most of the time we feel like no one cares about us.

"I'd like to share a few statistics with you. There are currently more than four hundred thousand of us in the United States. Think about that. That's almost half a million children. That is just about the population of the entire city of Raleigh. Wrap your head around that number for a second.

"Now, to make you think even more, at this very moment, in North Carolina alone, there are close to eleven thousand children in foster care. Eleven thousand. And there are fewer than six thousand licensed foster care homes. If you do the math, that means there are quite a few of us who don't get placed."

I paused for a moment and scanned the room. My gaze fell on mom, Maria and Erica were midway through the crowd. I saw Vivian seated not too far from them and Officer Burns was sharing her table. Wouldn't it be cool if Vivian and Officer Burns ended up together?

"So what happens to the kids who don't find a forever home? For all the horrible things that I lived through, I feel like one of the luckiest kids in the world. Even with all the fights I've been in, all of the abuse I've endured, it all brought me to the McClellands. Not every kid is that lucky. According to the research I have done, in 2022, fifty-three thousand six hundred sixty-five children were adopted from foster care. Their average time spent in foster care was twenty-two months.

"Almost fifty-four thousand children adopted sounds like a lot, right? That still leaves three hundred fifty thousand waiting for a home. During that same time period in North Carolina, just over thirteen hundred children were adopted from foster care.

"Every year, more children enter foster care, and every year the number of children adopted drops. The kids who aren't adopted end up aging out of the system. Roughly twenty thousand children age out every year. Imagine turning your child out at eighteen simply because they turned eighteen. The kids who age out of foster care are more likely to become homeless, become drug abusers, have difficulty with mental and physical health, and go to jail.

"I want to stress that I was one of the lucky ones. Fostering is hard work. I know I certainly wasn't an easy kid. The first night I stayed with the McClellands, I stole mom's wedding ring and ran away. She could have put me out, but she worked with me. She never gave up. If you want to foster and really make a huge difference in the life of a child, it is going to be hard work. But I can promise, it will be worth it.

"Oh, and one last thought. If the foster placement is not successful and the child is not going to end up staying with you, please don't send them on to the next home with their belongings in a trash bag. It seems like a simple thing, but when kids see that, it makes them feel like they aren't worth any more than the garbage being put out for pick up, like they are just another throwaway kid. Make sure they leave with their belongings in a suitcase. Trust me, it makes a huge difference."

I moved on from the statistics to tell the stories of the events I have lived through. I shared some of the stories of foster children I have met along the way. Some of my stories had the crowd laughing, some drew tears. I could tell that even the most hardened and cynical of the attendees in the group were touched by the stories I shared. When I was finished, I thanked everyone for taking the time to listen to me and I turned to leave the podium. As I turned, I saw someone I thought I knew.

At the very back of the room, just inside the doorway, I saw a tall, elegant woman wearing wool slacks, a silk blouse and fine gold jewelry. Her hair had been pulled back into a tight chignon. I hadn't seen or been close to her in over ten years.

Even across the room with all of the scents of the delicious food, I swear I could smell her perfume. I couldn't believe it. My grandmother somehow found out about this event and came to hear me speak.

I can honestly say I don't hate her anymore, I'm not even mad at her. I have made peace with my biological family and have learned to be grateful to them. I used to rage about her failing me. If she had been a better mother or grandmother I wouldn't have ended up in the system, my life wouldn't have sucked so bad. Now I am thankful for her. It is because of her that I have been gifted the amazing family I now have. I don't hate her, I feel sorry for her. The biggest loss is hers. She never got the chance to get to know me, and she never will which is sad, because I'm pretty awesome!

I walked back to my seat, gave mom a huge hug and thanked her for giving me a home and a forever family. I am no longer a throwaway kid.

ABOUT THE AUTHOR

Shannon Tessari is a psychiatric nurse in rural North Carolina, working with children navigating the aftermath of trauma—most in foster care or group homes, each with stories that are both heartbreaking and hopeful. Her days are spent amid the quiet resilience of these young lives, and her evenings with her rescued husky mix and her family.